# White
*on*
# White

ALSO BY AYŞEGÜL SAVAŞ

*Walking on the Ceiling*

# White
*on*
# White

Ayşegül Savaş

RIVERHEAD BOOKS

NEW YORK

2021

396 9518

RIVERHEAD BOOKS
An imprint of Penguin Random House LLC
penguinrandomhouse.com

The short story "Canvas" has been previously published in
slightly different form in *The New Yorker* (2019).

LIBRARY OF CONGRESS CATALOGING-IN-PUBLICATION DATA
Names: Savaş, Ayşegül, author.
Title: White on white : a novel / Ayşegül Savaş.
Description: New York : Riverhead, 2021.
Identifiers: LCCN 2020048284 (print) |
LCCN 2020048285 (ebook) | ISBN 9780593330517 (hardcover) |
ISBN 9780593330531 (ebook)
Classification: LCC PR9165.9.S28 W55 2021 (print) |
LCC PR9165.9.S28 (ebook) | DDC 823/.92—dc23
LC record available at https://lccn.loc.gov/2020048284
LC ebook record available at https://lccn.loc.gov/2020048285

Printed in the United States of America
1  3  5  7  9  10  8  6  4  2

Book design by Daniel Lagin

*For my parents, Neşe and Serdar*

# White
## *on*
## White

Mornings, the apartment expanded with light. Light flitted across the walls and curtains, streaked the wooden floorboards, lay dappled on the sheets, as if a luminous brush had left its mark upon my awakening.

From my bed, I could see out onto the small, trellised balcony, lush with the thick foliage and purple flowers of a clematis climbing up a stone wall. White geraniums lined the railing. There was a single forged iron chair and a round table.

Any personal items, if they'd once been there, had been cleared for my arrival. There were no clothes, jewelry, photographs. On the dressing table beneath a mirror stood a green ceramic bowl; in the hallway, the dark, rounded arms of the coatrack were bare.

Still, everything was marked with life, rich and varied. Each room echoed a story of unknown proportion, appearing and disappearing out of focus. The sparsity gave the place its character, so distinct and so fleeting.

In the year that I lived there, I had the sense of having stepped inside another life.

There were two paintings in the apartment. One was a small portrait of a young woman against a dark background. She was wearing a loose shirt with a flowing collar. She had an intense, feverish look and wildly gleaming eyes. The painting hung unframed in the hallway, by the stairs leading to the upstairs studio, to which I did not have a key.

The second painting was even smaller, almost a miniature, inside a black frame on the bookshelf in the living room. It was of a crooked tree on a hill, with fields rolling behind it. A wispy cloud hung halfway above the landscape. It was this painting that I looked at most often, gazing at its gray-green skies when I read in the evenings.

The apartment had been advertised in the news bulletin of the art history department where I was enrolled for my doctoral research. It was situated in the city's leafy eastern quarter, on a narrow road leading to a plaza. Yet the rent was low, even for my budget. I'd received a year-long fellowship to live in the city and travel to several cathedrals in the region central to my proposed study.

The owner of the apartment, a medieval studies professor, lived some hours away in a prestigious university town. He had announced the flat in various departments' newsletters with the expressed hope that it could be of use to researchers. I was well acquainted with the professor's work but had never met him in person; it was with his wife, Agnes, that I corresponded regarding my stay.

A student coming for a short term would suit her well, Agnes wrote to me; she was a painter and came to the city from time to time to meet with her gallerist. One peculiarity to our arrangement, she added, was that she would stay in the upstairs studio, with a bed and separate bathroom, whenever she came. If I didn't object, she would be careful to keep out of my way.

I was quick to take the offer and moved in some months later.

Within days of my arrival, I had adapted to the changing moods of the apartment, sitting on the balcony during the early mornings, moving my papers to the kitchen as the sun ascended, then to the living room. Afterwards I went out for a walk, the work of the day settling into place and gradually fading away.

The city was empty during my first weeks. Streets were filled with dried leaves of late summer, entangled with garbage, all of it drifting slowly like the long afternoons. Most restaurants and shops were closed, with fading paper signs saying that they would open for business the following month, though it did not seem to me that they would ever be open, that the city could be anything other than its somnolent shell. Those who had remained emerged from buildings in the evening, walking to the plaza to sit on the benches around the fountain, in weary disbelief that the heat had passed as the sunlight deepened to gold.

I walked as far as the northern hills, the southern walls, the cloisters past the old city gate, or followed the course of the river inland. I had the feeling that the city had known of my arrival and kept a space for me, whose precise shape and meaning I was yet to discover.

I was researching Gothic nude sculptures of the twelfth and thirteenth centuries. In my proposal, I argued that these nudes had largely been overlooked in art history. There were no studies on the iconography of the naked body in the Middle Ages nor any attempt to understand why the existing nudes—few in number, that much was true— were given place within the medieval culture of dense clothing. My plan was to spend the first months creating an inventory of nudity in medieval texts before traveling to the surrounding towns to see the sculptures themselves.

Throughout the previous year, my adviser had questioned my interest in the topic. My earlier studies, she reminded me, had focused on sculptures of mourners, from which I could easily build a solid thesis. She didn't want me to abandon the topic on grounds of originality—there was still much work to be done on mourning figures. She found my sudden interest in nudes too hasty, and reminded me that the medieval body in art was one cloaked by drapery; if I wanted to study attitudes towards nakedness, she said, I would be better off focusing my attention on all the ways that the body was hidden from sight rather than revealed. Medieval clothing was so symbolic, she said, that inspecting its different forms would elucidate notions surrounding various body parts as well. Nor did it seem to her that I was able to articulate a very original perspective with which to examine the few nudes at my disposal, abstract in their soft, curved limbs and their unspecified sex. Of course, if I insisted, she would sign whatever documents were necessary for my funding. But she wanted me to understand that there may not be much to investigate.

It was not the lack of originality that had led me to abandon my initial topic but the clear position that mourners occupied in medieval art. I wanted to research an ambiguous topic, whose greatest challenge would be one of consciousness: to view the naked human form as medievals did. Nakedness, in its purely physical aspect, was exactly the same for medieval and modern humans. Yet the perception of being unclothed might hold entirely different meanings, like a thin film obscuring the subject from view. In my studies until then, I'd felt confident in dates, periods, styles; I could make my way steadily through academic theories that cast each subject in a different light. But all this was an external framework when I had no impression of the internal force that propelled medieval life and art. I couldn't be certain that what I found beautiful, exaggerated, comical, or sad in the writings and art of the time had indeed been created with those sentiments.

There was no clear course of study for entering another's consciousness, historical or not. This was as difficult a task as undoing one's own mind, unraveling each layer of thought with all its prejudices and assumptions.

Early September, when signs of life were gradually appearing, I went to the gallery representing Agnes's work. I'd come upon a brochure of a past show in a drawer in my bedroom and wondered whether it could have been left there for me. I was curious about my landlord. The more time I spent in the apartment, the more I admired its sparse aesthetic. There was nothing out of place, nothing that called attention to itself in its restrained elegance.

I walked the hushed narrow streets of the city's chic northern neighborhood, lined with lacquered doorways opening to large courtyards, beyond which I saw the softly lit windows of stone buildings. Everything was deliberate, angled in a stern confinement, revealing only whatever was pleasing to the eye.

The gallery was bright. From a table at the far end, a

woman in thick, fashionable glasses looked up from her computer then looked back down.

The paintings hung sparsely in two rooms. I walked around, scanning the work for Agnes's name, not knowing what to expect. In her last message to me, checking that all was well with the apartment, Agnes had mentioned she would come to the city soon, to meet with a curator about a new series, inspired by medieval sculpture. She seemed unaware that this was my own research topic, and I could not recall whether I'd mentioned to her the specifics of my thesis.

I was surprised to come upon a series signed by Agnes of bright paintings depicting masks, stacked one on top of the other, covering the canvas in a patchwork of shapes. They looked like animal heads and demons, with horns and fangs. Others were human faces, their expressions sober, not giving away their emotion. The paintings' formal restraint held back a sense of bewilderment, which I felt residing beneath the tangle of images.

This, in a way, was my first meeting with Agnes.

After I left the gallery, I walked up a hill dotted by lampposts turning on in the half-light of the evening. The shops and buildings gave way to tall, dusty trees, bent over with their own weight. The steep road was strewn with garbage, jutting out of weeds and grass. At the top of the hill, I reached a small, rectangular plaza with a fountain, its glassy water reflecting the coins covering its marble base.

The city stretched between the hills, lighting here and there in an uneven melody, in brick and stone, high and low. I could make out the modern metal and wood spine of the library, built some years previously to the protest of the city's natives and the applause of architects. Next to it rose the stone pillars of the archives. Buildings squeezed beside colossal domes and the large lots of old factories. I thought of the lives stacked in crevices of the city, unraveling at every moment.

I spent early mornings reading on the balcony. Down on the street, people appeared alert to the new season, attentive to their surroundings. Later, I went inside to sit facing the painting of the tree in the living room. Sunlight moved from wall to wall. The city hummed mildly outside.

I wrote to my adviser about my initial observations from my readings. Nudes in medieval art appeared in moments of transition, most pronounced in depictions of the Day of Judgment. They were handled with concentrated attention, making them more real alongside the abstract, clothed bodies of saints and kings. The medieval artists sculpted the naked body as they did the forms of leaves and flowers, reflecting their frailty as well as their fullness of shape. These bodies were individual rather than symbolic, unlike those of bishops or angels. In sermons, too, flesh was described with visceral accuracy, though often in relationship to man's sins and ultimate judgment.

I'd been at the apartment for two months when Agnes wrote that she was coming.

I heard her from the bedroom late one evening. The door in the hallway opened and closed. She didn't call out to me before going up to the studio.

The following day as I was leaving for the library, I ran into her on the building stairs. She was tall and pleasingly thin. Her dark hair was tied back in a ponytail. She was dressed in a crisp white shirt, opening up into an elegant ruffle on one side of her waist, at once striking and casual. Her shoes resembled royal slippers and were the same soft shade of green as her trousers. She may have been on her way to the opera or to a bookshop and would have been comfortable in either place. She wore no ornaments, except for a rectangular gray stone ring on one finger, which I noticed when she extended her hand.

"You must be our tenant," she said. "Finally, we meet."

She enunciated each word, as if she were reading aloud from a book.

She was just coming back from a museum, she told me,

where she'd spent a long morning examining a single painting of a ship caught in a storm. She urged me to see the painting for myself, though she realized I must be busy with my research. I told her I would make sure to see it.

If I had time later, Agnes suggested, we could get a coffee together. I agreed enthusiastically and we set a time to meet at a café down the street.

"So long," she said, and raised her hand.

When I arrived at the café that evening, she was sitting at a table on the terrace. She had changed out of her outfit from the afternoon and was now wearing a light sweater and matching scarf. There was a book open in front of her, although it seemed, rather than reading, she was deep in her own thoughts while she stared down at the page.

"Is this alright?" she asked, pointing at the chair in front of her. "Everything feels so tightly packed in the city." She pulled the table towards herself to make room for me, looking me up and down as she did so, no doubt making a quick observation of my appearance and arriving at a silent judgment.

While I settled, a waiter came to ask for our order. I followed Agnes's decision to have a coffee, though it was already late. Her presence was magnetic.

Agnes gave our order in the same manner as I'd noticed

on the staircase, marking every word with textbook correctness. When the coffees arrived, she pinched the packet of sugar and shook it, then tore the tip and slid its contents onto her spoon, gradually pouring the granules into her cup and mixing slowly. I realized I'd done the same myself, slowly emptying the packet into my cup, even though I drank my coffee black.

"It's a strange feeling to be back," Agnes said. "I'm constantly shaken out of myself. Like this." She put her hands to the edge of the table and rattled it. Some of the coffee spilled onto her saucer.

Most of her recent work, she said, was formed around attaining stillness, letting the residues sift through until she obtained a blank mental state. She rippled her fingers in the air, drawing an invisible stream from top to bottom. The gray stone ring shifted around on her thin finger.

"It may sound useless, or just an excuse for doing nothing. But it happens to work surprisingly well in my case."

The process was like digging deeper inside a single moment, she continued. Within every state of silence, there was another, finer one. The more she grew attuned to it, the more she found places to explore within. Eating became slower, and walking, too. So much happened in the simplest acts that they were feasts to observe.

She sat still for hours each day, and when she worked, she found her vision crisp. For so many years she'd longed to be able to work like this, in command of the hours of the day, without distractions.

"But as you see," she laughed, "I seem to be starved for conversation. I'm going on and on."

It was fascinating to hear a painter's process, I said, and asked her to continue.

This prolonged period of observation, Agnes told me, was actually a training in morality. She was wary of letting corrupt thoughts enter her mind—be they thoughts of anger or envy or other, trivial things. It might seem like an abstract discipline, but it was actually very concrete: just as she wouldn't think of eating a piece of food that was rotten, she did not want to allow tainted thoughts to take up space inside her.

Of course, she added somewhat hastily, she didn't live in total isolation. There was her husband, Pascal, for one, whose ideas and presence nourished her painting in interesting ways. There were her children, too, a son and a daughter, though they now lived far away and didn't need her as much as she might assume.

"I don't want to seem like I'm cut off from the world," she said. I told her it hadn't seemed that way.

In fact, she continued, it was Pascal who suggested that she spend some time in the city and visit the gallery. She was grateful to him for considering such things. She appeared embarrassed after this admission, not in keeping with her poised manner.

She would stay in the city for a few more days, she told me, but added that I should carry on without making any changes to my routine.

The terrace had begun to fill up. Some tables were already set for dinner. The waiter came over to ask if we would be eating and Agnes asked him for the bill, paying for both of us before I had a chance to object.

We left the café and walked down the street to the building. At the door, Agnes said that she would continue walking for a bit longer.

I thanked her for the coffee, and the company. I hoped that we could have another conversation before too long.

The following day during my evening walk, I ran into Agnes on the street. Once again, she looked striking, in a green felt cape that flowed down to her waist. I asked whether she would like to walk a bit with me, in the park or by the river.

"That's a wonderful suggestion," Agnes said, touching my shoulder.

She pointed us in the direction of the plaza, adding that she was feeling rather tired. She'd been to the gallery that morning, then walked the whole way back. She used to walk the same route, she said, from up north to the city's heart, when she first arrived in the city as an art student several decades ago. Those northern neighborhoods were so foreign to her, then, and so alluring. She'd wanted nothing more than to belong in their world, though she felt intimidated by them.

It was difficult for me to imagine her being intimidated, I told her.

"You're really lovely," Agnes said, seemingly unaware of her own charm.

We sat down on one of the benches in the plaza. I asked about her meeting at the gallery.

They were happy with her recent work, Agnes told me, which she envisioned as a series of white paintings of the human figure, with expressions both serene and demented, like those seen in figures from the medieval period, whose naturalism astounded her.

Did she know, I asked, that my own research was about nudes of the same period? I hadn't considered that the extremes of expression in Gothic sculpture could be attributed to a naturalist sensibility.

"Then I must sound completely naïve to you," Agnes said. "I'm too quickly awed by the visual, and too eager to reproduce it in my own way. Mine is just the childish curiosity of an artist."

Both approaches, I assured her, the academic as well as the artistic, were important in their own ways, though I felt embarrassment at the conventionality of this statement.

"You're very generous," Agnes said. "I doubt that my husband would ever concede to the merits of the artist's perspective." In any case, she went on, the gallery wanted her to explore the topic further and she was glad to have a clear direction in her work for the coming months. The most important issue was attaining the deep state of concentration she'd described the previous evening.

I told her I'd been to the gallery myself; I wondered whether the paintings I'd seen on display were made in a similar state of meditation.

"No," she said, "those paintings are very old."

They belonged to a time in her life when she had just decided to be a painter, and set to work on the type of thing she thought of as painterly. This was part of her history in the city, when she was desperate to know what was considered tasteful. Thinking back, what she remembered most was how keenly she mistrusted her own judgment, and how much she'd set her intuitions and inclinations aside. The works I'd seen at the gallery were from this period, and she often had the sense that she had tricked people into accepting her as an artist.

"I hope," she said, "that you learn to trust your own tastes, in whatever work you do."

It was by chance that she started building on her own

work—the sketches that came to her without effort, in dream states, when her mind was elsewhere. She found them messy and contorted, and was bothered by their awkwardness, as if she were looking at photographs of herself as a teenager. In fact, her feeling for them was not unlike what she had felt towards parts of her body as a young girl—the secret worry that she was somehow deformed, the fear and awe of examining herself in private. With the sketches, as with her unknown body, she didn't know what was unique and what ugly; nor did she want to expose herself by asking for an outside opinion.

Once again, I found it difficult to imagine that Agnes could be self-conscious, that she'd ever felt ungainly.

It was the simple accumulation of these drawings that finally caught her attention, at a time when she had set aside her professional ambitions, or was tired of them. She was surprised to find that these sketches she'd been making for years were honest and alive, entirely different from her controlled paintings.

In the past, she'd spent many hours copying paintings at museums and she'd observed that what distinguished the work of the masters from their contemporaries was a lack of perfection. Perfection was produced externally, with the visual and tactile skill of a craftsman. Whereas the greatest art was dragged out from deep within and appeared disturbed alongside its flawless counterparts.

She had in mind a triptych, one she'd first seen with Pascal many years ago, whose focal point was the watchful eyes of the Virgin Mary. When I asked, she said that she could no longer recall the artist. Pascal would no doubt be able to tell me in an instant.

But that was beside the point, she added, when she could conjure every detail of the work. At first glance, the Virgin seemed out of proportion, her eyes too big compared to the rest of her face and too far up on her forehead, as if they were surveying the rest of the composition. But what became apparent, if you looked steadily, was that the eyes were alive, the face that of a human—not ideal or perfectly symmetrical, but someone you might have seen before, in a shop or on the street. In fact, it was a woman so real that it was hard to believe she could be the Holy Virgin.

Artists who could point out the human strain in our mythologies, Agnes said, were the ones who were capable of the deepest feeling. Once you'd seen that art had the ability to capture life at its most fleeting moments, it was difficult to be satisfied with a refined and frozen craftsmanship, as she had been for so many years.

Of course, she couldn't altogether abandon craft. Until

recently, she'd apprenticed with an art restorer who also taught classes in technique. He was very old-fashioned, the type of person who lived in another time, willfully ignoring the present. His studio was identical to ateliers of the nineteenth century, as was his vision of art. He worked only with oils, mixed his own paints, primed and stretched his canvases, fitting them with copper nails. He had no interest in the art of modernity, let alone contemporary works. But it would be inconceivable for him to consider that his unshakable belief in his own good taste was nothing more than a rigid wall protecting him from the chaos of life itself.

Actually, she said, she sometimes worried that she was too much like him, in her unyielding tastes. In any case, she'd been making reproductions of classical paintings at his workshop, which proved a good discipline in technique. In fact, her son and daughter happened to think that these reproductions were nicer to look at than her own work.

She let out a sharp laugh as she said this, and I turned my head to see that her eyes had welled with her own laughter.

Both of her children lived abroad and worked in areas— finance and consulting—that she knew nothing about. They, in turn, knew little about Agnes's work; what compelled her to do it, why she chose the subjects that she did. There'd been times, over the years, when she'd wanted them to ask, only so she would have an opportunity to tell them about herself.

"But what would I have told them?" she said, adjusting the cape around her shoulders and crossing her legs. Children had no interest in their parents' pasts, not really, especially not if the knowledge would make them uncomfortable or might force them to reconsider their own loyalties and resentments.

I didn't understand what resentments she was referring to and I didn't want to appear prying.

Similarly, Agnes continued, she'd never thought to question her children's choices or tried steering them in any one direction. Pascal, on the other hand, had been openly disapproving when their interests didn't meet his standards. He had always wanted them to be well versed in literature and art; he could not bear the slightest hint of their ignorance.

"You can imagine what he's like," she said.

I told her I'd never met Pascal, even though I knew and admired his work.

One time, Agnes had overheard her daughter saying to a school friend, nonchalantly, that her father didn't find her very interesting. This was many years ago, when her daughter had been a willful, clear-minded child. She and the friend were coming through the hallway to the kitchen, when the friend remarked on the number of artworks. "It's because of my father's work," her daughter said, which was true; Agnes never hung her own paintings around the house. And although the paintings weren't strictly part of Pascal's study, he always made a point of surrounding himself with beauty, harmonizing his mind and environment.

How lucky it must be, her daughter's friend said, to have such a father. With her own parents, it was nothing but schoolwork and house rules. That was when her daughter made the observation that her father wasn't very interested in her, probably aware that Agnes could hear. Perhaps she was waiting for Agnes to object, which she didn't. But she admired the bluntness of the statement, and her daughter's ability to keep this knowledge at a distance from herself.

Her son had been more guarded. Throughout his adolescence, he'd played a game of tug-of-war with his father, stubbornly defending his own choices and trying not to let on that he was affected by Pascal's opinions. Then as a teenager, he'd made a point of stressing his similarities with Pascal, taking an interest in everything his father did. Later, he started his own life and became an entirely different man. Agnes could feel her son's pleasure in his own autonomy, his newfound interests, as if they were meant as proof of something.

In any case, Pascal now admired their son's and daughter's modern, independent lives. He was enchanted with the way they presented themselves to the world, groomed and confident, and pleased at having raised children who were, in his words, so competent. He called them on the phone often, was delighted to hear about their routines, worried about the slightest obstacles. He told acquaintances about the children's lives as eagerly as he talked about his work.

Perhaps he'd only come to terms with their individuality once the children were sufficiently far away. Whatever the reason, both their son and daughter now had a close relationship with Pascal. Perhaps they'd even forgotten how much they'd once dreaded his judgment.

It all worked out, Agnes said, looking out at the plaza. At this point, it would be useless to confront Pascal about his change, to say that he didn't deserve the fondness of the children.

I was startled by the bitterness of the statement and wondered whether she really meant what she said. But I didn't wish to contradict her. I was aware of wanting her to feel close to me.

In a marriage, Agnes added after a moment, you had to let some things pass.

In the coming days, Agnes and I both stayed home, she upstairs and I downstairs. We ran into each other in the hallway or kitchen. On several occasions I asked her to join me for tea or to go outside for a walk. Every day she appeared in a different outfit, each one surprising: a long, pleated skirt; a dark velvet suit; blue jeans and a gray flannel shirt. I studied each one, as I studied the way she talked, the wine she bought for the apartment, how she drank her tea, trying to commit her tastes to memory. I didn't ask when she'd be leaving, not wanting to hasten her departure. I hoped to make the most of her acquaintance in that brief time.

One afternoon, Agnes came to the kitchen with a basket of fruits she'd bought for me at the neighborhood market.

Weekly from my balcony, I saw the market being set up and dismantled but had never been to it.

She took out different colors of plums from the basket and placed them in a bowl.

I'd spent the morning reading about the western portal of a nearby priory church, whose depiction of the Virtues triumphing over Vices was suggested to be the work of a famed stone workshop that had also made the sculptures of the city's cathedral.

"I won't get in your way," Agnes said, "I just came to give you these."

I was mostly done with my work, I told her, and asked her to join me. She sat down and began looking through the papers scattered on the table. One of them was written by Pascal. I'd read it many times, for its insights on the liminal spaces in the Gothic imagination.

"He's very proud of this one," Agnes said, picking it up. "He considers it one of his most original works." As I surely knew, much of Pascal's research in the past years had been a continuation of the same project of boundaries, the thresholds of good and evil, virtue and sin.

"I suppose it's good to focus on one theme," she said, "though I sometimes wonder whether he hasn't said everything he has to say."

Pascal's work was highly regarded in the field, I told her.

"Of course," Agnes said matter-of-factly. "I'd never question his authority."

Not long ago, she added, she'd accompanied him on a tour of northern cathedrals, to see different renditions of the wise and foolish virgins. The two of them stayed at bed-and-breakfasts, went on walks, immersed themselves in the northern landscape of green and stone that had been so formative in her own work. It was rare that she and Pascal traveled alone these days. From time to time, she joined his trips with students, though she often had the feeling that she was tagging along and that her views, if she expressed them, would sound simplistic. The students were friendly to her, making a point of sitting next to her at dinner, and she could not help falling into the role of professor's wife. She had known such women herself when she was a student. They were elegant and motherly, tending to the students with admiration while still considering them children. These wives told the students not to worry so much about their work, to get some rest, but listened attentively to the developments in their intellectual paths, never doubting that great things lay in store for them. Back then, it would not have occurred to Agnes that the women might not really be interested in the students at all but were highly skilled in their performance.

Anyway, she said, Pascal's most recent work was about the sculptural representations of the wise and foolish virgins in Gothic art and stemmed directly—she pointed at the table—from the paper I'd been reading. I hadn't known about this last strain of his work, I said. It sounded fascinating.

"You must be familiar with the parable of the ten bridesmaids," Agnes said. Five women remembered to bring oil for their lamps while the other five forgot to do so. When the bridesmaids were summoned at midnight for the wedding, the foolish ones realized in panic that they had nothing to light their way and asked the others to share their oil with them. But the wise women left the foolish behind, and followed the bridegroom to the wedding. The lesson to be learned was that you must always be prepared for the Day of Judgment. But what sort of lesson was this, Agnes wondered, when the women were deemed wise for their smugness and their unwillingness to share? How were they judged fit to enter heaven, when they had left their desperate friends behind?

She'd always been bothered by this story, which was why she was particularly moved by one cathedral on their recent tour, where the ten virgins stood in almost identical dress, with echoing features, as if they were indeed the same woman.

Whatever moral the tale wished to emphasize about vices and virtues was undone with the sculptors' empathetic portrayal: it was clear that the women were wise or foolish out of no fault of their own, and that their fates could easily be reshuffled any which way. Besides, the foolish ones might even have been more sympathetic—their shy smiles revealing a deeper humanity, unlike the haughty grins of the virtuous.

Pascal thought that Agnes's interpretation was entirely wrong. In fact, he was irritated with her, going so far as to lead her one by one past the ten statues, pointing out all the differences that marked the women as separate and that declared a rigid morality carved deep into the sculptures. He drew her attention to a certain flare of cloth, often used in depictions of the Holy Mother, for example, or the foolish women's headdresses.

Agnes didn't challenge him, though she doubted that the men and women entering the church all those centuries ago would notice the minute folds of cloth suggesting vice and virtue, rather than a line of young women who were equal in their loveliness and humanity. It was much more likely, she thought, that they would take in the perfect curve of the foolish virgin's toe peeking out from beneath her dress, its innocent plumpness communicating a simple and immediate virtue, rather than any symbolic sin hidden in her gestures or the wrinkles of her clothing.

"Pascal should never hear me say this," she said, smiling slyly. She sometimes had the impression that he was dismayed with her opinions on art.

I told her that I agreed with her interpretation of the statues. I didn't think in the least, I added, that her reading of art was superficial.

Still, she went on, the trip had been a very pleasant one, despite the disagreement. With fine food and wine, she said. There were villages whose streets were lined with flowers, each with its unique products and crafts, proud as if they were the only one of their kind in the world. They stayed in quaint thatched houses, went on boat rides on the river, tasted the local foods.

"Just the two of us," she said.

She raised her palm to one side of her head, patting her hair lightly. She got up and said she would go up to the studio. She hadn't yet started on a new painting, she said. She was hoping that very soon she would get to work.

As she was leaving the kitchen, she stopped and turned

to face me. She'd spoken to Pascal on the phone that morning, she told me. The two of them had agreed that it would be best if she stayed in the city for a bit longer. Both for her sake and for his. If I objected, she could certainly arrange to stay someplace else.

I didn't mind, I said. In fact, I was glad to hear it, even though I did wonder what it was that kept her away from her marriage.

My first trip outside the city was to a cathedral in a small town east of the city. I left the apartment early in the morning and was planning on taking the last train back in the evening.

When I arrived in the town, I made my way towards the steeple rising dramatically above the town, visible beyond the pizza and kebab shops surrounding the station.

The square was empty. At the far end was the ornate clock tower whose image was often printed on postcards of the region. On one side of the square, a line of colorful, latticed houses stood brightly facing the white stone.

I had seen reproductions of the cathedral in many textbooks and could easily identify individual sculptures on its façade. Still, I was surprised by the building's size and the teeming portal: the solemn jamb figures enveloped in robes, the Death and Assumption of the Virgin along the lintel, the radiating voussoir of angels, prophets, and kings holding up their hands in witness and prayer. Above them were the watchful eyes of demons and beasts, their narrow skulls staring wildly in every direction. The animated wickedness was all the more striking alongside the calm faces, untouched by the spectacle of evil twisting and turning right beside their heads.

It was like the sight of an ocean frozen in full swing, waves of a hundred sizes. The harmony of the composition was at once felt and impossible to discern. Staring up at the portal, I felt the shudder of a silent and controlled music, sprung out and held in place, round and narrow, high and low, the notes of the intricate stone ringing in perfect balance.

I had borrowed a folding stool from Agnes and set it up in front of the north transept to observe the sculptures of the Day of Judgment. I wrote descriptions of the nudes one by one in a notebook, as many of them as I could make out. I would take photographs once I'd recorded my immediate observations. I listed the infant-limbed bodies, rising from their tombstones or huddled mischievously in a corner. I couldn't tell whether they expressed fear or surprise, if it was with ambivalence or joy that they approached the moment of their own judgment. Their malleable bodies looked guiltless, and had no appearance of finality. Nor did it seem, though the facts of the narrative were clear, that they were in the last moments of their existence.

I went inside the church, which was entirely empty, to eat the sandwich I'd prepared the evening before, then lay down on the pew. I must have slept for over an hour. When I woke and left the church, inky clouds were drifting with quickening pace across the sky, dragging the late afternoon with them. I walked through the winding backstreets of red and yellow brick. My hands had grown numb with cold. Most of the restaurants and shops were closed, and it was not clear whether there were times when the town came to life.

As I was thinking of going back to the station to wait for the train there, I spotted an antiques shop in an alleyway. Inside, a woman sat half-hidden by the clutter, a shawl spread across her knees. She looked at me without expression then continued to gaze out at the street as before. The shop was crammed with porcelain: tea sets, platters, tureens, cake stands decorated with deer and foxes, oak trees and daisies. Long, squat, round, and square bottles lined one wall, chiseled with leaves and fruits, all of them remnants of another world, governed by a different set of manners that survived behind the shutters of the town with dignified resignation. I went up to an oil painting hanging high on a wall. It was of a country road at dusk. Two children were walking towards a house in the distance, their hooded heads tiny beneath barren birches. It was a similar evening to the one about to descend on the town. One of the children in the painting seemed to be cradling something hidden from sight. As I stood looking at it, the old woman suddenly came to, shuffling her legs, and told me that the painting was not for sale.

At the last minute, I decided to change my ticket and stay in the town for a few more days, at a hotel next to the station. I had no plans, except to visit the cathedral again at different hours. I was there early in the morning, when the nudes of the Judgment appeared all the more alive, lit by low rays. Cathedrals were receptacles oriented to catch the light to greatest effect. It was important for me to consider not just the sculptures themselves, but their various characters throughout the seasons.

The day of my return to the city, there were delays and it wasn't until late in the evening that I was back in the apartment.

The next morning, just as I'd begun comparing my notes of the nudes to the ones in reference books, Agnes came into my room. I was sitting on the floor, my notes spread around me.

"There you are," she said. "It's felt empty in the apartment without you."

While I was away, she'd changed my bedsheets and put a pitcher of flowers on the dresser. I considered telling her none of this was necessary. I was a bit startled to find my room tidied and uneasy at the thought that Agnes might have noticed that my sheets were unchanged since the time I'd arrived at the apartment. I thanked her for the flowers and the clean linen.

"It's nothing," Agnes said. She sat down on the chair at the foot of the bed. There was something invigorating about sharing a work space with another person, she went on. She could almost feel my project's influence on her own. Not that she knew too much about it; she hoped that I would tell her more about my readings, the ideas I'd begun to assemble from my research at the archives.

As a student at art school, she continued, she'd shared a studio space with a girl named Claire. Then, too, she'd felt another person's work communicating with her own. Claire's paintings were harsh and exciting. Their vague shapes were of sinewy, tangled bodies, from whose crevices emerged the heads of fish and flowers. Not unlike Claire herself, who looked like she'd been wound up and might at any moment unravel into a wild being. Agnes's work, in comparison, was dull, with its everyday objects and scenes.

Claire's father was a painter as well, and her mother, too. At least she seemed to come from an artistic background, judging by her style. She and her husband frequently visited the studio and talked about their daughter's work with perfect ease. Agnes had never shown her paintings to her parents and she couldn't imagine that they would have something to say about them. Sometimes, Agnes said, it frustrated her that Claire had nothing to prove, nothing at all to work out in her life as a painter.

From time to time, Agnes saw Claire with one of their instructors, a man named Peter, having coffee in the school courtyard or chatting in the print room. He was tall and thin, dressed in neat, matching clothes. He must have been in his thirties, though he reminded Agnes of a precocious child. He'd recently shown his work at an important gallery. Among the paintings on display was one of Claire lying on a bed, wearing her studio trousers and a black shirt, unbuttoned halfway. Tubes of paint lay scattered around her on the bed.

Peter had never shown recognition of Agnes's presence beyond a quick nod or a passing remark. He was silent during weekly critiques, listening to other instructors' comments and at times offering a grunt of agreement or distaste. Regarding Agnes's work, the tutors all agreed that her earlier style had been too simple, lacking sophistication, but that it was finally beginning to show maturity.

In the home of Agnes's parents was a painting—the only one—of a girl holding a basket of red and purple flowers, whose colors were only somewhat darker than her round cheeks. The girl wore a straw hat and a striped dress with round buttons running up its fitted top. Her smile was broad. A dab of white paint in each pupil was meant to convey her delight. Agnes had spent hours of her childhood examining it, enchanted by the girl's beauty. It occurred to her that the instructors were objecting to the very part of herself that marveled at this painting, scrutinizing her provincial tastes.

One time, after the tutors left the studio, Claire told her that she admired the simplicity of Agnes's work. She wished she could make such straightforward paintings herself, full of unrestrained emotion. Agnes saw things more clearly, she insisted, with nothing twisted or hidden.

At the time, it hadn't seemed that Claire was paying her

a compliment, when Agnes's only wish was to twist and complicate, to hide firmly from sight the person she'd been.

She was alone in the studio one evening when Peter came in. He glanced at Claire's corner, though he seemed to know that he wouldn't find her there. He came to stand behind Agnes, looking at her painting above her shoulder. It was of two young men shown in three-quarter profile, the composition inspired by a painting she had seen at the national museum. She went to the museums more than any other student, studying dates and names, trying to memorize all that was considered good.

In her painting, the two faces were rigidly mannered and it was impossible to tell what they might be feeling.

"Very good," Peter said, pointing at the hidden mass of one of the figures' heads. He told her that he, too, favored the concealed profile above all others. He was working on such a portrait himself and invited her to see it.

As the evening was setting, they walked to his studio some streets away from the school. Claire lived in this neighborhood as well, in an apartment her parents rented for her, so that she could walk to her classes. Claire had suggested that she and Agnes live together the following year—they could easily find a bigger place and Agnes wouldn't have to take the two buses that brought her to school from the dormitories—entirely oblivious to the fact that Agnes could not afford to live in an apartment; her parents could barely pay for her room.

In one corner of Peter's studio was a nude sculpture, which Agnes thought must be a replica of a classic Roman one, though she hesitated to say it.

"Isn't she exquisite?" Peter asked, turning to look at her. His face was framed by his turtleneck sweater riding all the way up to his small, round chin. Agnes was aware of disliking him, though the feeling didn't mean very much, even to herself. She became aware, also, that she felt ill. She took a step back, turning her attention to the easel, on which stood a small painting in darkened profile. The slender features, Agnes supposed, of Claire's face.

Peter was still looking at her, keeping his eyes steady even when she turned her head, so that his gaze became dramatic.

"You must know," he said, "what an effect you have."

With girls like Claire, he continued, you would quickly find out what sort of imagination lay beneath their mysterious features. It would be messy, dramatic. But he believed that he and Agnes shared a similar sensibility. He'd known it all along and could finally see it now in her new work.

Agnes felt a warmth between her legs and the ill feeling overwhelmed her. She was wearing light trousers and made an excuse to leave, hurrying out of the studio.

It must have been her swift departure, she concluded afterwards, that sealed her allure. The thought was intoxicating, as if she could attain anything else she desired with equal ease, simply by walking away.

The following week, Peter was waiting for her in the supply room behind the studio. Agnes had already decided that she would go along with whatever followed. She had no previous experience, nor did she think she would enjoy herself. Rather, she saw the process like a task, a destination she'd set her mind on.

She went to Peter's studio again some days later. In the daylight, the portrait appeared different. The angles of Claire's face were exaggerated and menacing. It wasn't a truthful painting, Agnes thought, nor was it even very skilled.

They took off their clothes and lay down on the bed behind the easel. Peter was very thin, with purplish skin. He moved with stiff exactness, as if his muscles were cramped.

Agnes had the sense that he was gliding over her, their bodies never quite meeting.

When she left the studio at dusk, he asked whether she was feeling alright.

"I'm keeping you from your work," Agnes said to me. She was sitting upright on the chair, her hands on her knees like a schoolgirl.

I had a new vision of her, self-conscious and insecure, different from what I was accustomed to. Perhaps I was feeling irritable that day, and tired from my journey.

She used to think, Agnes said, that there were winners and losers in friendships, just as there were in romantic affairs and marriages. The score might change over time, fortunes might reverse, but it was always the case that points accumulated on one or the other side. Although it was impossible to know, even later, whether she had ever succeeded in gaining an upper hand in the friendship.

"But we were just girls," she said to me, as if the memory had just made sense to her. These days, as her daughter liked to remind her, the correct term was *women*. But really, Agnes said, they weren't women at all. And she'd never been able to admonish the young, eager girl that she'd been for her desperate effort to be alluring, for trying to make her way.

In any case, Claire had gone on to enjoy considerable success in her career. She'd abandoned painting and became known for her sculptures of everyday objects, polished and rounded to perfection. What made the works interesting was their slight tilt, the ordinary world rocked off-balance.

That same week, Agnes came down to the living room to stretch a canvas. She had brought a stack of wooden bars and a roll of linen and was trying out different configurations for the boards. She had a shape in mind, she said, narrow and wide, like old engravings of city panoramas, though she didn't yet know what she would paint on it.

The weather had turned but the apartment was not sufficiently heated. I sat on the couch with a blanket, facing the painting on the bookshelf; the tree in the picture appeared more crooked each day. Cold, damp air streamed through a small crack beneath the window.

I'd recently read about the production of parchment from animal hides in the Middle Ages and I was thinking about skin—as a device for transcribing narrative—a possible lead in my research. At the archives' special collection that week, I had looked through several scrolls relating to diseases and their cures. Around the holes and slits where the parchment had ripped, one scribe had made doodles of gaping mouths and genitalia. Before I left, I made a note about the relation between touch and narrative, both of them acts enabled by skin. Human flesh, of course, had long been linked with knowledge, most obviously in Adam and Eve's expulsion from Eden. Skin, as a vessel for writing, was the very embodiment of knowledge. And cathedrals were decorated with the lush iconography of the body for those who couldn't read.

That morning, Agnes told me, she had talked on the phone with her son, who'd shared some of his worries about his girlfriend. She was not an easy person, and couldn't control her temper when they had a disagreement. For the past few days, he'd been walking on eggshells, without quite knowing what offense he'd committed.

It was difficult for her to hear such stories, Agnes said, without harboring animosity towards the young woman. She and Pascal would meet her soon enough, as they did many of their son's girlfriends, because he liked to invite them home on holidays. Their son patiently introduced each new partner to the routines of his past life, even though none of his relationships ever lasted for very long. On their first evening in town, they would go to the pub where her son had worked as a student. The following day, they'd go rowing, or meet old friends from school. After dinner on their final day, they all entertained the girlfriend with family stories, teasing and contradicting one another, creating occasions for rehearsed jokes. Agnes often bought presents for the young women—shawls, books. She did this against her better judgment, because her son appreciated the attention shown his partners.

Pascal had an effortless way of drawing the women in. He complimented their ideas, even asked for their opinion on some aspect of his research, as if they might provide a point of view he'd never considered. Later, when the relationship was over, he was the first to say that the young woman had not been a good match, and that he had seen this from the very beginning.

Agnes continued arranging the stack of wood for the frame, even though she had already tried out every configuration.

"I wonder what you would think of my son," she said. She guessed that he was the type of person I might get along with—quiet and attentive, never quick to judge. Sometimes, she found it a shame that she could not simply be friends with her son and daughter, rather than having to tend to them as a parent.

"Just as I am with you," she said, smiling. With her children, she would never be able to have conversations like these. I was pleased to hear this. Even though I'd been considering going to my room to continue my work, I stayed sitting on the couch.

Since the first years of their marriage, Agnes continued, Pascal had been certain that they would eventually have a family. Agnes chose to be silent about it, figuring that once enough time passed, the idea would naturally dwindle. What she remembered most from those first years of marriage, before they had children, was the pleasure of life. It was the first time that she'd felt confident in the city. She'd just had her first exhibition, and looked forward to meeting people, proud in the flush of her small success.

They were friends with a group of young artists, and their gatherings were opportunities to compare themselves to one another. The parallel developments of their lives held them together in a semblance of community. Agnes could no longer remember whether she genuinely liked the company of the group, but she looked forward to each occasion, to drawing people's attention.

She was accustomed, Agnes said, to being told she was beautiful; she almost expected it. At the time she would have insisted, falsely of course, that she didn't care about the compliments. But beauty mattered to her. It was one of her ambitions, even more ardent than her painting. Women guarded this particular desire, didn't let it seep through publicly. What Agnes wanted above all was to perfect herself, as if she were in perpetual bloom.

"But you should know," she said, "that there comes a time when your body begins to give way. And you should also know that this happens very early on.

"I'm not talking about the inevitable, serious problems of old age," she continued, "all the medical routines and treatments, continuing life with daily pains and pills. I mean the sudden loss of weightlessness which you get accustomed to in your youth."

I told her I couldn't quite relate to what she was saying. Not that I felt leaden, I said, but I could feel the weight of my body the way I assumed everyone did.

She lifted up a wooden bar and stood it vertically on the floor. She asked me to hold it in place while she fitted another one, forming a corner.

"I can see that you still feel the illusory freedom of your body," she said. During her own years of perfect freedom, she'd suddenly begun to feel ill, taken by a sly disease that morphed under her skin, unable to be detected. She was tired, she was in pain. She complained of cramps, of head-aches, of her body burning as if it were on fire. She would decide to ignore it, to focus her attention outside, and for a while the pains would subside, until she was taken over again by fatigue.

Every doctor she went to found something slightly wrong, though none could quite say what the matter really was. Nor did she know what the body must feel like as it ma-tured naturally. Was constant, sly pain a normal existence, or was it a muted cry for help?

It was during this time, as she paid meticulous attention to her body, that she began to notice she was aging in mi-nute ways—one or two gray hairs, sun spots on her hands, the slight bulge of her stomach that was nonetheless shapely. She panicked at the sight of each new feature, fearing that the change would speed up all at once: her hair would turn gray in the course of a year, her skin grow suddenly dull and saggy. Daily, she scanned her body, listening to it in pure meditation. It was alive with burning, aching, morphing decay. The beauty and confidence she had only begun to harvest was just as swiftly being snatched away.

"You should also know," she said, looking up from the floor and the pile of wood, "that there comes a time when the main challenge of your life crystallizes in a matter of months. A pain or fear manifests itself at the exact moment when you lose your sense of youthful weightlessness."

In fact, she continued, it could be said that the precise shape of a person's fears took form on their first encounter with their own decline.

"You're still some years away from what I'm telling you," she said. "But you will certainly arrive there." I shrugged. It didn't seem to me, I said, that each person reacted in the same way to their mortality. Still, I offered, it was an interesting idea and I would be fascinated to see the embodiment of my own fears, like the chimeras of the Gothic imagination.

"Fascinating isn't the right word," Agnes said curtly. For her, she continued, the challenge had been to continue to live her life, rather than focus on her imminent fall, as if she'd reached the edge of a precipice. She had wasted years focused on the pains of her body, waiting for disease to take over. Which it never had; at least not as she'd expected. What took shape, instead, was terror.

There was a dream she'd had repeatedly in those years. In it, she was covered in hair. Hair grew down her neck, her torso, crept up her cheeks. She would wake up drenched in sweat, certain that her body was under siege, and bring her hand to the nape of her neck thinking that she would surely rub against bristling fur.

Looking back now, she saw that she was likely experiencing a crisis, and searching to fix it in roundabout ways.

"And that's the story," she said loudly. "That's why I had children."

It had seemed unbearable to go on with her life, experiencing her own steady deterioration. She wanted to give it up, all at once; she wanted to silence the minute deformations dramatically, to put an end to her own torment. She had no desire to continue their carefree life—the spontaneous gatherings, the small daily competitions—once she felt that it would end, sooner or later. She'd push her fears to their very limit; would throw away her precarious beauty and freedom, give it all up to another.

She rolled out the linen canvas and smoothed it with her hand. She placed the wooden frame on top, folded the cloth to cover it, and began to staple, alternating from side to side.

"I tell you these stories," she said, "and I can't tell whether you want to hear them."

I found her stories interesting, I told her.

"Interesting," Agnes repeated after me.

She'd stapled the canvas all along the wooden frame. She picked it up from the floor and turned it around. She'd done a messy job; she'd been talking too intently. The cloth was unevenly stretched, bulging in parts.

"In any case," she said, "you're an excellent listener."

It wasn't often, she went on, that we could present ourselves to others, like a self-portrait. More often, we made portraits of the people around us, guessing at their features from occasional glimpses.

My days were determined by moments when the heavy rain slowed to a drizzle, allowing me to walk the short distance to the bus stop or go to the library. Some afternoons, after the library closed, I walked around until dinnertime then ate at a café.

I was reading widely on medieval perceptions of the skin. Given unsophisticated methods of surgery in the Middle Ages, the inner layers of the body were still shrouded in mystery. The skin itself was seen as a blanket, stretched to cover a secret inner life. And what did this thin blanket signify, I wondered, beyond its ability to conceal.

One week, I took a day trip to see a surgical treatise, in whose marginal illustrations a figure had taken off his skin as if it were a jumpsuit, and stood naked in a second layer of tighter bodily matter. It wasn't entirely necessary for me to see it—I might not even use any of it for my thesis—but I was glad to spend time away from the city for a few days. The treatise was housed at a castle an hour and a half away by train. I had a letter of introduction from the head archivist in the city and was taken to the library on the upper floor, dim in the purple-tinted afternoon light filtering weakly through stained-glass windows. The librarian drew my attention to another text she believed might be of use, having misunderstood that I was writing on medieval attitudes to disease. It was a treatise on leprosy as a manifestation of diseased morality. Thus, the writer concluded, the skin was a mirror of inner virtue, though it could also be argued that the leper was a test of faith and of the human capacity for mercy.

Two weeks after our conversation in the living room, Agnes invited me to the cinema with her. I hadn't seen her much since then because I was mostly out of the apartment during the day and went straight to my room when I came back. We met at the theatre entrance in the early evening.

She was wearing a plum-colored silk jacket. Long gold earrings touched the sides of her bare neck. She must be cold, I guessed, but hadn't wanted to spoil her outfit with a scarf or heavier coat. She'd already bought the tickets, she told me when I turned towards the ticket booth. It really was the least that she could do.

"I'm sorry I've been here so much longer than planned," she said, but she didn't mention how much longer she would be staying.

The film was about two women who fell in and out of love with the same man, over the course of one summer at a beach house. The three characters arrived and left the house at different moments and combinations, while the tension among them escalated to the point of a silent eruption.

It was raining heavily when we left the theatre. We ran to the bar next door and sat at the counter; neither of us had brought umbrellas. The bartender, who'd nodded at us when we walked in, watched Agnes settling on the stool in front of him. Slowly, she took off the silk coat darkened with the rain, revealing her thin, bare arms. He was still looking at her as he filled our glasses. I hadn't realized, though I wasn't surprised, that I wasn't the only one to examine Agnes intently.

It would be so strange for her children to see her, Agnes said, spending time with someone their own age. As I probably knew, it was difficult to think of one's parents as individuals, to imagine them capable of regular conversation. But there was something more to our acquaintance, so detached from both of our usual routines. Didn't I think, she said, that our conversations existed on a separate plane?

I nodded in agreement. It had been good to spend some days away from the city. I was glad to see Agnes again.

She'd had such a friend once, Agnes said, a woman named Eva whom she saw daily, even though they had no other social bonds. She'd met her soon after her son's birth, when she and Pascal moved to the town where they still lived, for Pascal's position at the university.

Agnes was at the charity shop in town one afternoon, where she'd wandered with the baby to look through stacks of china plates. She used to give herself small tasks, to give some order to her days. It was commonplace to say that those early years of child-rearing were difficult ones. They'd brought her life to a halt and it seemed to her that there was no way out, that life would pass with a constant effort to get through each day.

There was another woman at the shop that afternoon, looking at a pram for sale, her own baby strapped to her chest.

They left the shop together and went to the main street for tea, upon the woman's suggestion. It was as if she had decided they would be friends and was speeding up the first, tedious steps. They talked about the babies' feeding, their sleep, their different ways of fussiness. Eva told Agnes that she dreamed one day of having a café of her own, describing with unabashed childishness the pastries she would serve, the color of the walls, and the tables. Agnes could picture it perfectly, littered with knickknacks and framed words of inspiration; the type of place that she'd never think of going to.

Back in the city, her friendships had been defined by restraint—how little you gave away, how much you managed to suggest about yourself without revealing the mystery. The artists she was acquainted with never talked openly about what they were working on, at least not until the moment of their realization. Her friendships with other women similarly functioned on concealment: desires weren't articulated until they were achieved. It was not only the fear of failure that kept them in shadow, but the shame of wanting, as if their yearnings would strip them of their poise.

Eva herself resembled her exuberant imaginary café. She had brightly dyed red hair, wore outfits of swirling, splashing patterned dresses. The type of woman, Agnes guessed, who was at ease with her body and took pleasure in it. She seemed at once wise and naïve, able to accept the harshest judgments calmly, but breaking into a giggle at the slightest provocation.

On that first meeting, she asked Agnes questions without hesitation or embarrassment: how much had their house cost, what did Pascal do for a living, did Agnes make money from her work? When they were parting, she declared that they should meet again soon, perhaps go for a walk. They could motivate each other to shed the extra pounds of their pregnancies. She slapped her hands on her thighs, indicating what needed shedding.

Agnes had finished her drink. She looked at mine, still half-full. "I'll get another in the meantime," she said. She pushed her glass towards the bartender, her arm taut and luminous in the dim light. He met her eyes and filled her drink. He also brought out a bowl of nuts, which Agnes nudged in my direction.

That year, the two women met up in the mornings to walk around town or go to a café. Some days, she went over to Eva's house after her husband left for work. Eva lived several streets away from her and Pascal, in a small house, with a walled garden where there was a plastic table, a barbecue, and many pots of plants among the dry grass.

They sat outside on sunny mornings or on the sofa in the kitchen, where, it seemed to Agnes, there was a perpetually singing kettle. She felt more comfortable there than in her own home. Even on her first visit, she'd kicked off her shoes and pulled her feet under her on the sofa; she felt no discomfort when Eva went around preparing things; she even enjoyed asking her for more tea, for an extra cushion, a blanket for the baby, not out of laziness but for the pleasure of intimacy.

They were in the thick haze of motherhood together, as if a cloud had descended on them, and perhaps for this reason they talked about everything: routines and daily pleasures, past relationships. Eva liked to bring up her disappointments in life, from the smallest to the greatest, mentioning them side by side as if they were of the same scale. She regretted that she'd painted the walls of the house white, when she could have chosen something livelier; she regretted that she did not have an education. If she'd gone to university, she said, she would probably be in the city now, living her life alone.

Most days while the babies slept, Eva cooked lunch and dinner, putting aside half of whatever she made for Agnes to bring home. Her kindness was steeped in justice, which she doled out without a second thought. She offered Agnes practical advice, gave her clothes and dishes she no longer needed, and easily asked for things in return.

She'd never felt so familiar with anyone, Agnes said, outside of her own family. The pleasure of spending time with Eva was what she imagined it must be to have a sibling. She didn't worry about Eva's judgment; she made no effort about her appearance or the particular ideas she put forth, as she had done with her friends in the city.

"You have to remember," Agnes said, though I didn't

recall her telling me, "that I met Pascal so soon after I left home. So soon that I hardly knew who I was."

Pascal had crossed paths with Eva once or twice. He wondered why Agnes spent so much time with this woman who seemed, he said, not very interesting. Those days, he offered periodically to find a nanny, so that Agnes could get back to her painting, as if he supposed Eva's support came in the form of childcare, rather than friendship.

"I wish I had a photograph of her to show you," Agnes said. "But I don't think I ever took one."

There'd never been an occasion for that: she and Eva never saw each other on holidays or special celebrations, even when the babies turned one. Their time together had never become part of their greater lives, even if it consisted of the most tangible intimacies. She did have some drawings back in town. Even though she painted rarely at that time, she used to sketch Eva in the kitchen. One was of Eva feeding her son, the shadows behind her merging with her unruly hair, in contrast to her neck and open breast.

It was such a friendship, Agnes said, to last her an entire lifetime.

Perhaps the only point of tension between them was that they never got together as couples, even though Eva invited them often for barbecues or weeknight dinners. Agnes always made an excuse, knowing Pascal wouldn't enjoy it. Maybe Eva knew this as well, because she would joke about Agnes disappearing back to her mysterious life after each meeting.

One morning, Eva told her that her husband had had an affair with a woman at his work. He and the woman had been on a trip together; the whole thing had happened one night without plan. Her husband was full of remorse afterwards, and had come clean immediately.

She cried as she told Agnes the story, and Agnes held her in the kitchen, the babies asleep beside them. Agnes now remembered how happy she'd felt. Full of strange joy that she was the one offering Eva comfort.

Afterwards, they walked towards the lake. It was the same route they took on mornings when they managed to convince one another to go out, rather than sit in the warm kitchen. That afternoon they continued past the lake, to where the tidy streets of bricks, cars, and bicycles gradually shifted to the majestic trees hiding grand houses. Everything was tinted green. Soft moss on the pavement, thick hedges delineating plots, ivy lacing stone. This was the neighborhood where Agnes and Pascal lived, and it made Agnes uneasy to walk that path. She'd never invited Eva to her house, with the excuse that Pascal was often home in the mornings. It embarrassed her to think what Eva would make of its display—the books and paintings, all the signs of their learning and wealth.

Eva used to play a game picking out her favorite houses, listing everything she would do differently if she owned them. Her changes usually involved conveniences for her child and husband. She'd put up a swing, build a pool, a patio for the barbecue. She didn't understand, she said, why these people lived such closed-off lives, shut away in their beautiful homes.

As they were passing a house in whose front yard Eva had once included a play area for her son, Eva told Agnes that she could understand her husband's side of things. Surely, she held some little part of the responsibility.

It was a topic Eva came back to daily: the orientation of her body towards her child, her diminished desire. In the past, she'd felt confident about her husband's desire for her, certain that it would remain. Perhaps, she'd once said, this was why she'd been drawn to him in return. She didn't say that to belittle her husband, she continued. On the contrary. Women who schemed endlessly to keep a man's attention seemed pathetic to her, and misguided in their frantic effort. Agnes mostly kept silent, though she flushed with the accuracy of her friend's observations.

In the weeks that followed, Eva seemed to have come to terms with the event and she simply let the matter go. She was even glad, she said, that it was out of the way. Surely this was the type of crisis that came along in every marriage.

At every meeting, Agnes pushed the topic further, searching in her friend for some reserve of anger, a desire for justice. Their morning conversations revolved around the same debate. Agnes insisted that it was a matter of dignity, of Eva's self-worth, even though she knew that she was pushing it too far. She had no interest in trying to understand her friend. She only wanted Eva to see the situation as she did and to regard her husband with the same contempt that Agnes felt for him.

By the time Agnes's son and daughter were in the care of a young au pair, the two women saw each other only occasionally. For a year or two, Eva ran a pastry stand with another woman from her son's school. Agnes stopped by from time to time for a coffee, though it was awkward to let the women treat her to it.

Agnes had invited Eva's son to her house on several occasions, to play with her children. Eva had been admiring of the house, without judgment or bitterness. Agnes couldn't remember why she'd thought Eva might feel uncomfortable. Maybe that was just her own discomfort all along. She'd baked a cake—more decadent than her children were normally allowed, the type of thing she imagined Eva bringing to school events. Another time, she prepared colored clays for them to mold. She and Eva chatted in the kitchen, though never with the ease of their earlier friendship. Both times, there had been a fight among the children and it was an embarrassment for the women to soothe them without taking sides.

After the birth of her second child—whose first months Agnes had not at all been a part of—Eva and her husband moved to a new, modern suburb on the outskirts of town. So there was really no drama, Agnes said, to the way their lives drifted apart. Perhaps it had been inevitable.

It was not clear to me why Agnes had said that this friendship was similar to our own relationship, but I didn't ask, fearing a long explanation.

I pointed to my empty glass and suggested going home. Agnes placed a bill on the counter and put on the silk jacket. By the time the bartender had prepared the change, she was already waiting for me outside.

It was the end of November. Mornings were damp, the mist hanging low, as if the city had been struck by a slow forgetting. The flowers of the clematis on the balcony had disappeared. I sat in bed, looking out the window, still inside the territory of the dream, the same one I'd had since arriving in the city.

In the dream, I heard my name called out, again and again. The voice came from a place right beside me, though I couldn't see the person saying it. I thought I should get up and walk to the adjacent room, where I was sure I would find someone. They could have been a stranger, or someone I knew intimately. I'd wake up with a wish to call out to them.

I spent the rest of the morning at the library, recording individual figures that lined two cathedral portals in adjacent northern towns; they were angels and demons, the holy and the damned. It was slow, meticulous work, blurring my sight so that everything on the carved stone appeared entangled with one another.

The human form was distinct in sculptures of the thirteenth century, looming ever larger within the space earlier reserved for the forms of nature. But human figures still carried the traces of flora, as if they had emerged from the thick of woods. Twigs and fingers, branches and limbs. Hair curling like fronds. Medieval men and women would have delighted in identifying the species turned to stone—hawthorn, oak, rosehip—and I wondered whether they may have felt a similar delight in seeing the body as well, examining all the separate parts that they, too, were made of.

I photocopied pictures of individual sculptures and spread them on a long table, staring at the tangle of shapes, then grouped them by various characteristics: depictions of sinful flesh, of the body in pain or in pleasure. As my inventory grew, it seemed that these attributes blended into one another, that there was little distinction between what was desired and what was shunned.

Afternoons, I went to the park in the city center, at the hour when bushes and hedges were lit golden at the tips, as colors everywhere else darkened. Wide tree trunks, cracked and mossy, gave way to the lawn, stretching brown with a lush decay. High up, the bare branches were chiseled against the dusk sky. Rooks sat unmoving at the tops like paper cutouts, their raw evening calls the very sound of the deep season.

Agnes had been living upstairs for almost two months. I would hear her in the studio or notice that she'd been in the kitchen when I was out. She always left something behind for me—a book, a note asking how I was, snacks. Except for this, we didn't communicate daily. I would go straight to my room when I came back home, or if I heard her coming downstairs. I assumed she preferred to be alone as well.

One afternoon as I was coming back from the library, I saw her sitting at the neighborhood café, with the stern-looking woman I'd seen at the gallery. I assumed the woman must be the curator. In front of them on the table were books and papers. The curator was taking notes on a small note-pad. I paused for a moment to watch Agnes as she talked with graceful animation, moving her hands expressively. She had been restored to an earlier self, the one that had enchanted me all those weeks ago, and I felt certain now that she was aware of the effect she had on her audience. The curator looked absorbed; perhaps she was even intimidated by Agnes. I walked away before Agnes saw me. It would have been an embarrassment for both of us, I thought, that I'd seen this enactment of her persona.

The following morning, before I went to the library, I left a note in the kitchen to ask if she'd like to get together. As soon as I was back home, she called to me from her studio.

She was sitting on a stool, dressed in leather boots and a tweed vest, her hair pulled tightly at her nape. Two long pearls dropped just beneath her earlobes. She looked as comfortable in her fitted outfit as if she were wearing a loose artist's smock. When I walked in, she swiveled towards me on the stool but didn't get up. Finally, she extended her hand to hold mine. I thought that the gesture, like her outfit, was planned, even practiced.

She'd started the painting at last, she said, but she seemed to be going nowhere with it. She pointed at the canvas in front of her, placed on an easel.

The painting was entirely white. The color was made up of different textures and shades—flat, round, cold, and warm; tinted blue or yellow, with lighter and darker shades. The head that emerged in the middle looked like a deity with its sharp, inquisitive features, though it was too faint to grasp its full form, as if I were seeing it behind a rapidly shifting mist.

Everything about the head had the sense of incompleteness—not of a fragment, like the remains of a fresco or statue, but of evolution. It seemed as though the figure, barely distinguishable from the blank canvas, was growing in parts and disappearing in others. Its shape was at once voluptuous and transparent.

"I set myself the challenge of painting only in white," Agnes said. "But I don't know how else to continue." She'd hoped that this one would become the first of a series, though now she doubted if she had anything left to explore. She placed the canvas on a ledge, high up on the wall behind her, and pulled out a chair for me. She sat back down on her stool.

"It may be nothing more than a gimmick."

I didn't know whether she'd called me up to show me the painting or if she even wanted to hear my opinion. In any case, I didn't know what I thought of it and hesitated to say anything. I sat down on the floor beside the easel.

The studio was mostly bare. A small metal trolley was stacked with painting supplies. At the back of the room was a sink, an electric kettle, and a burner. There was a box of cereal, crackers, and tea. A carton of milk was wedged on the corner of the open window. Against one wall was a narrow bed. I guessed that the cupboard along the back wall contained the remainder of Agnes's belongings.

I told her she should feel free to use the kitchen, adding that I hardly ever cooked.

These days, Agnes said, she didn't much feel like cooking herself. She often gave up at the simple thought of what she might make, even though preparing a meal had always come naturally to her, never with the sense of duty or dread that others might feel. She enjoyed it fully and didn't feel any sort of sacrifice in the act. Nor did she pretend otherwise, to receive praise or acknowledgment from her children and husband. It was something she'd learned from her mother, who had been a competent and generous cook.

Among the strongest memories of her past, she went on, was watching her mother in the kitchen. She would sit with her, chatting, while her mother moved from one task to the next, listening to Agnes's stories, maybe giving her something to do. Agnes had tried revisiting this place in her painting—that blue kitchen of her childhood and adolescence, which was both a physical and an emotional landscape: the round table draped with yellow cloth, the stiff white curtains, jars of flour and grains, chipped and broken utensils, which were never replaced or thrown away but adjusted to, with particular ways of handling them, as intimate as probing inside one's own mouth.

But she'd known from the very beginning that the place could not be represented with images. The objects of the room and her mother's stout figure would depict an era, a way of life, a social class.

Besides, what she remembered most of all was something intangible—her mother's gestures and instincts in handling food, the security of their time together.

"It was a direct line of communication," she said, though she and her mother had never expressed it as such. She noticed these days that the silent language of food had become a proclamation. People talked about food to satisfy another hunger, perhaps one for connection or even a sense of self.

Whenever she was visiting home, Agnes's daughter said that she wanted the two of them to cook together. The deliberation of it struck Agnes as odd. It was obvious that they would cook—how could they not?—but the statement made it forced, if not artificial. Her daughter suggested lengthy recipes for foods that carried an idea of old times: jams, pies, roasted meats. She took photographs as they cooked. Once or twice, Agnes had come across these photographs on her daughter's social media pages, with a line or two about the mother-daughter bond.

She didn't know how to point out the insincerity to her daughter, who was part of a generation of educated women that paid rapt attention to the things that gave them pleasure and turned them into rituals for display.

"That's a crude way to say it," she added. "I don't want to sound embittered."

These women, she went on, were indignant about any criticism regarding their exquisitely curated lives. Her daughter, for one, would defend the luxuries of her life as necessary ways of caring for herself. Taking a bath, buying a dress, going out to a restaurant were all considered therapies for the soul and its small wounds. The simplest acts, Agnes thought, the very fabric of life had spun out of proportion, expanded to grotesque magnitudes of egocentricity, just like old paintings, restored with too bright colors, that lost the subtleties of their initial expressions.

She brought a hand to her earlobe and tugged on the drooping pearl.

Still, she told me, she'd never share these thoughts with her daughter out of fear of alienating and upsetting her. Her daughter would probably say that Agnes was trying to

silence her, as so many women and their needs were silenced. This was a point her daughter brought up often. It
made her uncomfortable, Agnes said, because she was almost certain that her children knew very little of what it
meant to be truly voiceless.

Her daughter might also point out that it was healthy
to talk about oneself, to look deep within, in order to un-
tangle the traumas she'd carried since childhood. If Agnes
were to tell her daughter that she had grown up with no
real traumas, she would probably be told that her own point
of view was informed by a lack of introspection, by everything Agnes had silenced within herself.

There was no arguing with her daughter, she told me,
because disagreement could only ever point to Agnes's own
blindness.

She paused and looked at me. I could tell she was waiting for me to agree with her, as I often did, to tell her she
was neither blind nor mistaken. But I didn't feel it in myself
to say it.

Sometimes, Agnes continued, she had the sense that
her daughter did not quite consider her own mother a real
woman. And despite her daughter's insistence that women
should love and honor themselves with all their flaws, the
type of woman she must have had in mind was pleasingly

vulnerable, easy to console and embrace, whereas Agnes was rigid, and cold.

The room brightened dramatically with a parting cloud. Agnes turned her face towards the window and closed her eyes.

"I keep talking and talking," she said, her eyes still closed. "I talk and I talk and I don't know what you're thinking."

It sounded, I said, simply like a generational difference.

Perhaps she was just old-fashioned, Agnes said, but it seemed to her that severe introspection was a sure way to get lost in the smallest issues, to reduce one's life to a list of grievances. For her daughter, it felt like every conversation, every memory could lead to an injustice that needed talking through.

She should add, Agnes said, that she and her daughter had a very good relationship. They enjoyed many of the same activities, had similar tastes. Her daughter called often to ask for Agnes's advice on various things—strategies at work, what to wear to events, worries about her health. Agnes knew intimate details of her daughter's friendships, what they talked about, the comforts and envies of each situation. And she was proud of their intimacy; she didn't want to risk losing it by being critical. Whenever her daughter

shared her painstaking analyses—such as the fact that the
two hours she'd once spent sitting alone after school, waiting
to be picked up, was the cause of her anxiety at work—Agnes
would quickly tell her that she was sorry. With anyone else,
she would have found it impossible to apologize so quickly.
But she gave her children whatever they asked, not to spoil
them and not with any great passion, but so that they would
go on with their lives. A desire to avoid conflict with them
was even greater than any need to get to know her children
fully.

She got up from the stool and went to the window. She
removed the carton of milk wedged in the window frame
then continued looking out. From where I was sitting, I
couldn't see what scene she was following as she strained
her neck. Then she put the kettle on the burner and placed
a tea bag in a mug. When the water boiled, she steeped the
bag with deliberation, pulling up and releasing the string.
She added the milk and brought me the mug, then brought
out a packet of biscuits from a drawer.

In many ways, she went on, her own mother had been a
stranger to her. She couldn't say with certainty what sort
of life her mother had hoped for in her youth, what disappointments she'd harbored. It may seem cruel to renounce
intimacy with a parent, to state that they were strangers.

But wasn't it better to acknowledge your own ignorance rather than claiming insight?

Anyway, that life was entirely in the past, now. Her own son and daughter had no attachment to Agnes's hometown; they'd spent their childhood summers by the sea, each time at a different cove in a different country. They had no sense of where they came from. She didn't necessarily mean that as a complaint, though it was curious to her that her children evaluated each place they arrived in by its comforts and beauty, rather than the memories they'd accumulated there, let alone any sense of responsibility they may feel towards it.

Sometimes, she felt that there was nothing in her children's lives that was not beautiful. No ungainliness or embarrassment, nothing they wouldn't show the whole world with pride. Perhaps that was why her daughter talked so easily about her insecurities, because they didn't truly make her insecure. Of course, Agnes said, she would never tell her daughter this, either.

She got up from the stool and picked up the painting, tilting it from side to side. Seen from below, the figure appeared in free fall, traversing the layers of white.

"It makes me frustrated to look at it," she said and put it on the floor.

Part of her excitement when she started the painting was how naturally it progressed. She thought at the time that this had something to do with her mental clarity. Now, she wondered whether it was only the elation of working easily, without challenge.

The threshold between complete immersion in a work and being fed up with it was so slight, she said. Often, she didn't even notice that she'd crossed it until she found herself stifled.

"There is always the same enthusiasm at the start," she told me. "Just like the way you might initially present yourself to a stranger, with eagerness and curation. Even if they'll soon discover for themselves that you are made up of your vices and self-doubts. Very soon, they will see the person they first met is actually a stranger to the one who has taken up her space."

And yet at each new meeting, just like at the beginning of each work, there was the brief illusion that this one would be special, and that it wouldn't fall prey to the same shortcomings of every other relationship.

Agnes was standing in front of the building, wrapped in a dark blue shawl that swallowed her thin shoulders, twisting and folding luxuriously around her torso. It had been a long day at the archives: I'd gone through the illustrations of eleven books of hours from the northern region. The majority of historiated initials represented women in supplication. I considered extending my survey to include other books of hours or psalters, with the hope that this might provide a different insight into the depictions of women's bodies, albeit clothed. Still, as the archives announced closing time and I packed my notes to leave, I had the sense that I had wasted my day and veered off topic; that rather than expanding the avenues of my research I should focus on the depictions of nudes at my disposal, even if they were overwhelmingly of male bodies.

Agnes appeared to be looking for something in her bag and I thought she must have lost her keys, but I noticed when I came closer that she was holding them in one hand.

"Back from the archives?" she asked. It was true that I didn't have much variation to my days. Still, I was taken aback. I wondered whether she'd been waiting for me at the door, guessing the hour of my return. Beneath the blue shawl, she was wearing a long purple wool coat. A red scarf was knotted at her neck. Even though the colors were striking, they were also unharmonious, as if she had chosen her outfit in the dark. In fact, her appearance suddenly struck me as disturbed.

She suggested going to the café next door.

Hadn't she been on her way somewhere, I asked.

"Not really," Agnes said. "I thought I'd just step out for a little and then I ran into you."

Again, I wondered whether she had been waiting for me to come back.

"Just a quick coffee," Agnes said. "But feel free to tell me if you'd rather not."

Alright, I told her, but I'd need to get going soon.

"Did you have plans?" She may have been calling me out, or she may have asked in all sincerity.

I told her that I did, indeed, have plans, though all I had in mind was to be back home, in my room.

At the café, we took the same table we'd sat at on our first meeting.

She ordered a black coffee and asked for milk on the side, though she didn't pour any into her cup once it arrived.

She asked me if I'd had a good day. I was too tired to tell her about my findings. I said that I'd gotten a lot of work done.

"You're so productive," she said. "I envy your discipline." She, on the other hand, had been distracted all day, fiddling with the white painting. In the afternoon, she'd finally decided to put it aside for good and begin something entirely different. She would get to work tomorrow, or the day after.

It had happened once or twice before, she told me, that she'd felt so detached from her work and could find no way of relating to it. At those times, too, it had taken a while to make her way back to the surface and see things afresh.

After the birth of her children, when every day passed in a flurry of activity, the small and repeated tasks consuming days and months, she'd come to view her paintings as belonging to another person, someone who probed the world with curious superficiality. In the time that passed, with nothing more than ideas for works and a handful of sketches, she'd begun to doubt that she had anything of worth to communicate.

What did it matter, she wondered, the fruit placed on the table, showing off its angles and colors in a perfect assembly, the landscapes, the interiors, the bodies, and all the forms close to abstraction that provided momentary relief from the world?

Her paintings appeared rigid to her, even meaningless, though they had done well in her absence. Her gallery encouraged her to continue on the work she'd been doing before her children were born, as did Pascal. His own research had continued steadily through the children's births, without the slightest obstacle to his routine.

It was Pascal's idea to hire an au pair—a distant relative of someone at his department—who would live with them for two years and take over the children's care during the day.

Agnes consented, even though what she'd wanted from him was to take a step back and reevaluate their lives, rather than rush to make things as they had been before. When speaking of the toll of motherhood, women pointed to the time that was taken from them and never quite given back.

But what was lost was also the capacity for selfishness and single-mindedness. Agnes wanted Pascal to share in this loss, for the two of them to let go of their work and to pick it back up in time, after they'd come to terms with the shock of what had happened to them.

The top of Agnes's head was illuminated by the golden evening light. I noticed that the thin strands of hair, pulled back as usual into a low ponytail, barely covered her scalp. She brought her coffee cup to her chest, held it there for several seconds.

The au pair, Jana, arrived on a rainy weekend. Standing in the hallway beside her suitcase, she looked as if she would burst into tears. Pascal's colleague had told them that Jana was more mature than her years; she'd recently graduated from university and was taking some time to decide what to do next. But it seemed to Agnes that the stranger at the door was really just a child. She asked to go up to her room at once. After an hour, she emerged having changed into baggy, colorless clothes, looking as if she'd prepared herself for arduous physical labor. She barely spoke that whole day, though she listened carefully to the instructions given her: what time the children had breakfast, what time they needed to be picked up from nursery school, what they ate for snacks.

Jana responded vaguely when they asked what she preferred to eat, if there was anything missing in her room, if she'd like to have a bicycle. Those first weeks, she didn't join conversations during dinner but she sat with them the entire time. Agnes supposed the girl must be homesick or very shy; other times, that she despised them. It was also unclear whether Jana liked the children. But she supposed, Agnes said, that it was naïve to expect real affection from a stranger hired to work for them.

One Sunday morning, Agnes's son appeared in the kitchen and asked whether Agnes knew that an angel resided on his right shoulder and a demon on his left. If only he focused hard enough, the child continued, he could hear what they were saying. He closed his eyes and stretched his arms in front of him, as if he were walking in his sleep. "It will be a stormy day," he finally proclaimed. "And then sunny."

Pascal was reluctant to confront the au pair, insisting that their son had probably made up the whole thing. Anyway, Pascal said, there was no need to cause trouble when Jana was finally warming up to the family.

It was Agnes who talked to her, when Jana came home after her day off. They all wondered what she did on those days, slipping out before breakfast and not appearing until dinner was off the table. Agnes didn't think the girl had any friends. The shops in town were closed. She imagined Jana sitting alone on a bench, wandering aimlessly around town, just so she could be by herself.

The anecdote about the angel and demon, Jana said, was something she'd heard when she was a child herself. The children weren't even scared, she insisted. But as Agnes explained to her how such a story would no doubt be startling, would deform out of proportion into a nighttime army of chimeras, Jana began to nod. Alright, she said bitterly, she'd never tell such stories again. In fact, she would never tell the children any stories but only read from the books that Agnes selected.

"That's not what I meant," Agnes said, though she was aware that the argument had already shifted off track.

From time to time, Agnes went into Jana's room with renewed determination to act motherly, to soothe out whatever troubles the girl harbored. She told Jana that she wanted to know more about her and tried to recount amusing anecdotes from her own day. The girl sat silently at the edge of her bed, cheeks flushed crimson, as if she were being unjustly scolded. She answered all of Agnes's questions without offering anything more, as though determined not to reveal any part of herself—out of fear, or stubbornness, it was hard to tell. It was on one of these evenings that she asked Jana, having gotten nowhere in conversation, whether she could paint her portrait.

"She was extraordinarily beautiful," Agnes said to me. "Did I already say that?"

She swirled the pitcher of milk on the table then finally poured a few drops into her empty coffee cup.

For some reason, they all took pride in the girl's beauty, as if Jana had chosen them as her friends and her good looks meant something about them as well.

To Agnes's surprise, Jana agreed immediately to having her portrait painted. The following day, she sat in front of the easel, hands stacked on her lap. She posed as still as a rock, as if she were a trained painter's model, her eyes fiercely introverted.

Agnes worked slowly, over several weeks, building outwards from Jana's eyebrows, which formed a slight crease above her nose, her wide, tinted cheeks, her pursed, proud mouth. The face, as it emerged, did not so much reflect her beauty as it did her reserve, the frown of suspicion as Jana studied her painter.

"She gave me the chills," Agnes said. She added, also, that the girl thrilled her.

―――――

In the two years she lived with them, Jana always had a project to which she dedicated herself with discipline: memorizing monologues from plays, looking through art books, reading dated classics she couldn't possibly have been interested in.

If the children wandered into her room during her free time and asked to participate, she would firmly ask them to leave. It was admirable, Agnes and Pascal remarked, how seriously she took on the task of educating herself. Pascal lent her books and sometimes sat with her in the evenings quizzing her, delighted by the girl's dedication to whatever he gave her. Jana was more at ease around him, even joyful. She sometimes brought the children to campus from the nursery, and the four of them walked back together after Pascal finished teaching.

Agnes had noticed, when she went into the girl's room to bring her flowers or fresh linen, that Jana painted watercolors in a small rectangular notebook, the pages crammed full of sketches. There were the objects of her room, the neighborhood streets, drawings of children that resembled Agnes's son and daughter.

Agnes looked up from her cup and studied my face as if she were looking into a mirror. "Perhaps she was the reason I went back to painting seriously," she said.

Not necessarily because of the time Jana afforded her, but out of rivalry with the young stranger in her household, who spent almost as much time painting as Agnes did. Eventually, Jana began working on larger sheets and later on canvases, all of which she propped up around her bedroom, perhaps for Agnes to see. She was annoyed with the girl for painting so much, considered it dishonest, maybe because Jana had gotten the idea from her, or because she'd never asked Agnes for help.

"You'd think," Agnes said, "that she was in competition with me."

Still, she continued, it was a happy time, those two years of living with an au pair. This was when they settled into the rhythms of being a family, with an order to the way they lived their lives. In the presence of an outsider, their dinners were livelier, their affections softer. They teased each other and made up endearments, hoping to enchant Jana and catch her attention. Agnes remembered that at that time she even set the table with greater care, thinking to light candles, put out cloth napkins. She might prepare casual desserts, though this was not standard in their family, or cook something involving ritual and various steps—a pitcher of sauce on the side of soup, shells to crack, a recipe from fleeting seasonal vegetables—as if they had always enacted these traditions. Pascal was confident, the way he was around students, and more charismatic than Agnes had ever known him to be at home. And whatever Jana might have felt about them, it was always clear that she watched them greedily.

Something else, Agnes now remembered, was that Jana began to dress like her. It didn't happen all at once, nor was it unexpected. Agnes had given the girl many clothes—ones that no longer fit her, others that she considered too youthful. The first time, she asked Jana to look through some bags and take whatever she wanted from them before she brought the rest to the charity in town. The girl took everything. Agnes was flattered, and assembled more things. Jewelry, scarves, bags. There were items she gave Jana even though she still wore them. She felt satisfaction in her own generosity and the acknowledgment of her good taste each time Jana accepted her things. But her generosity was no different from her pride. It was not out of kindness that she gave Jana those things, but a pretense of it.

The girl wore Agnes's clothes in surprising configurations, with pieces that had never belonged together. She made them eccentric yet alluring, as if she were playing the role of Agnes in a film.

It was during this time that Agnes began her series of portraits, starting with Jana, then her husband and children and other acquaintances who sat for her. She no longer had any interest in professional models; she only cared to discover the people she knew through her paintings. But the cold and expository style of these works, whose faces were made up of a network of bulging veins, had worked most startlingly for the portraits of the au pair and the foreignness of her face.

Their friends often observed how much Jana had changed while living with them, from a shy, unremarkable child to an assured young woman. She should be grateful to Agnes and Pascal, they said. By this time, Pascal had convinced Jana to apply to the art history department and had more or less arranged for her admission.

It happened abruptly that their life together came to an end and Jana moved to a campus dormitory to start school. Within days of her departure, Pascal found someone to take her place as a nanny. The children were upset for a day or two, but quickly adjusted to the older woman who came several days a week, bringing them home from school and preparing their snacks before leaving in the early evening, when Agnes would be done with her work in the studio. Jana didn't come over for dinner, or for weekend outings.

The essence of a relationship often became apparent with separation, Agnes said. In Jana's case, it was evident that the girl had been neither family nor a real friend. Once or twice, Agnes had seen her on campus. She had grown at once fuller and finer, though she looked no more confident than that first Sunday afternoon when she'd stood, forlorn, on their doorstep. One time, Agnes had cycled past Pascal and Jana, eating lunch at a park adjacent to the campus. They were glowing, Agnes thought, immersed in what appeared to be an animated conversation. Or perhaps it was simply the ease they had in each other's company. For a moment, it seemed that Agnes was watching two strangers. She hadn't known that the two of them kept in touch, though she probably could have guessed it. She didn't slow down.

Agnes looked down into her cup, with its shallow pool of milk.

She remembered all this recently, she said to me, because of a conversation she'd had with her daughter. On the phone a few days ago, her daughter mentioned that the topic of the au pair had come up in therapy. Agnes was skeptical of the things that emerged at her daughter's therapy sessions, which often suited her daughter's immediate needs and urges particularly well, but she was nonetheless startled by this particular memory.

How was it, her daughter asked, that this young girl had lived with them for so long even though Agnes deplored the girl's presence? And why had Agnes never said a word about it, choosing, instead, to be willfully blind?

I asked Agnes what her daughter had meant by that.

"You see," Agnes said, "I was just as puzzled. She was on the verge of tears on the phone, but I didn't really know what exactly she was referring to."

She kept her eyes lowered on the cup.

"There was nothing she could have witnessed," she added. "I'm quite sure of that."

Her daughter, now crying, went on to say that what she remembered most of all was the terrible constraint of that time, the fear that her mother might suddenly be angry, even though she appeared so calm. The fear that their lives might shatter. It was only now, her daughter said, that she could look back on those years and wonder why Agnes had chosen to react as she did—silent and resentful—knowing that this would only hurt her own children.

"She couldn't bring herself to speak very clearly," Agnes told me, "and I didn't want to push her."

Before hanging up, her daughter asked whether Agnes remembered the way she used to calmly fold her napkin in the middle of dinner, then suddenly excuse herself. What did she want to say to them in those moments, as she and her brother waited in trepidation for a disaster that never arrived? And she wondered now, with the therapist's probing, about the au pair's disappearance from their lives, the smooth arrangement of her removal without a scene.

"But it wasn't a disappearance at all," Agnes insisted, as if she were trying to convince me as well. "The girl had figured out what she wanted to do with her life and she got some help from Pascal to achieve it.

"Surely you know how these things go," she said, "when professors pull a few strings."

Then all at once she raised her hand to summon the waiter.

In scholarship, monasteries and convents were often compared to the transitional space of a womb or to the threshold of death, the moments of human life that permitted nakedness. To live the enclosed life of a monk or nun was also to see the world from the margins. How strange the lives of the fully clothed must have seemed to them: the kings and queens carved on cathedrals in thick drapes, the jesters and merchants, all preoccupied with ornaments and constantly concealed by costumes and mores, by a rush of activity—what they called life, the brief interval between states of nudity.

By the time I returned to the neighborhood one late afternoon, the sky was darkening in smoky blues. It had been a dazzlingly cold and sunny day. The sky was high, the trees now bare.

I walked as far as the cloisters south of the apartment; there was a winter market set up at the entrance. I treated myself to almond cake and hot wine from one of the stands.

That morning, I had received an e-mail from my adviser about my first two chapters. I was well on track, my adviser wrote. I would have no trouble moving forward. Still, I should be careful not to veer too much off topic in my examination of nudity as a metaphorical state, especially in my evaluation of natural forms as yet another appearance of nakedness in medieval art. I was pleased that my months of research were paying off.

As I was entering the building, I glanced up to see Agnes watching from the studio window and waved at her. Since our last conversation at the café I hadn't heard her leaving the apartment. She called to say hello when I entered, then came to the living room after a few minutes, where I'd sat down with a cup of tea.

She was holding a large wreath of dark leaves, tied together by thick blue string. She'd come with an offering, I thought uncharitably, to retain my attention.

She held the wreath up to the window. We could hear the wind whistling through the windowpanes. It got dark so early now, Agnes said. She missed the light. Missed it deep in her bones. When the weather was like this, she had no energy to work. She had done nothing today but tie the leaves together.

I didn't point out that it had actually been very sunny all morning and afternoon.

"Maybe here?" She set down the wreath on the low table. She placed a brass candlestick in the middle and fitted a white candle on it. I went to the kitchen to get a cup for her as well, and poured tea for both of us.

"Don't you have other plans?" she asked. "I feel like I'm constantly disturbing you."

I'd already made the tea, I said; she should help herself

to some before it got cold. It was true that I had been avoiding her in the past weeks, because I wanted to focus on my work. But my adviser's encouragement that morning had lifted my spirits.

We sat across from each other on the sofa and armchair. I added that the wreath looked nice on the table. It wouldn't have occurred to me to decorate the apartment, though it brought about a pleasing awareness of the holidays.

Her mother, Agnes said, was one of those women who decorated every nook, especially in this season. The top of a television set and the washing machine; every shelf and corner. The house was crammed with cloths, baskets, dried flowers, and trinkets—an array of objects meant to communicate the idea of a home.

"You know," she said, "Pascal was shocked the first time he visited my family's house." She'd known it from his silence, his sudden reserve upon their arrival.

The two of them had been living together for several months when they took the train to her hometown. By then, she'd allowed herself to believe that Pascal's admiration for her would never falter, no matter what else he might discover about her.

When I asked, Agnes told me that the two of them had met at a cocktail party, following a lecture. Agnes was there with other artists, but she stood somewhat apart from them, because she didn't feel that she belonged to their group. Whereas Pascal had supposed this was because she was more refined, more confident. He'd told her this afterwards and Agnes hadn't suggested that perhaps he was mistaken in his impression.

"I often have this effect on people," she said. "I seem more self-assured than I really am. I'm told that I can be enchanting on first meeting, all the more so because I appear distant."

She was looking at me intently. I kept silent and looked away.

Anyway, Agnes continued, she'd told her parents nothing about Pascal, except to say on the phone that she would bring him along on her next visit.

Her mother had prepared the table in the dining room, reserved for guests, instead of the kitchen. It was apparent that she had spent the previous day cooking: there was more food on the table than they could possibly manage to eat, some of it placed simply for the sight of plenitude.

"There's so much food," Pascal said when he saw the table, and it wasn't entirely clear whether he meant it as praise. It had never occurred to Agnes, not until then, that hospitality might be something to rein in; that it was pitiful to offer too much, to display your enthusiasm without restraint.

When they sat down to eat, Pascal was sullen, answering her mother's questions briefly before returning his attention to his plate.

He was hesitant to talk about himself. Yes, he enjoyed his studies. No, he didn't see his parents very often. Agnes's mother cheerfully pressed on with her questions, pretending not to notice that Pascal resisted her interest. Her father was mostly silent, and exceedingly polite. When Pascal went upstairs, Agnes told her parents that he was very shy.

"So it seems," her mother said, and her father said nothing. In fact, her father never said anything about Pascal in all the years that followed. When she told them a year later that they would get married, he asked only whether she'd thought it through.

Upstairs, Pascal was lying stretched out on the bed. His suitcase was unopened on the floor. He hadn't even taken out the gifts he had brought for her parents. Agnes didn't ask him what he'd thought of them and Pascal didn't offer any observations.

He told her that he was puzzling over something he was preparing for a symposium. He couldn't work on it there, he said, without his books and a proper desk, and had decided to leave the following day after lunch rather than staying the entire weekend as they'd planned. He went to bed early, after going downstairs to tell her parents that he was too full to eat dinner, as if eating were their only means of communication.

The two of them spent the following morning walking past the town to the fields and farther into the bordering forest. The air was cold and fresh, the grass stiff beneath their feet. Agnes showed him a favorite tree at the forest's entrance, the paths and clearings of her childhood. She took him to a tangle of branches that wove together like a dome. All that time, she had a sense that she should not have brought him there, neither on the walk nor to her home, though she knew, also, that she would not confront him about any of it.

By the time they returned to the house, Pascal was as she'd known him in the city, full of observations and eager to hear hers, showering her with admiration. He was even cheerful around her parents, perhaps now that his time there was almost over.

Her mother had set the table in the dining room once again, with a whole different set of foods from the previous day. Pascal gave them the gifts he had picked out with care back in the city: a leather book cover for her father, a silver candle snuffer for her mother. They seemed out of place in that house, too refined among the rest of her parents' belongings.

She'd known all along that Pascal had imagined her home differently: a country house, her parents spending their days tending to their books and flowers. The type of life he was accustomed to. She hadn't thought to correct him; perhaps she didn't want to. But she sensed his surprise at the small brick house, the carpeted bedrooms, the moldy bathrooms.

In the months that they'd been together, he was almost delirious in his enchantment with her, and certain of her good taste and judgment, more than she had ever been certain of herself. It was as if, in his despondent mood upon arriving at her parents' house, he wanted Agnes to acknowledge that there was something wrong, to assure him that she was indeed as he'd imagined her to be.

Again, Agnes looked at me intently, as if the story she was telling was meant to communicate something to me directly. I asked whether Pascal had gotten closer to her parents in the following years.

He'd been back to her parents' home only a handful of times after that, Agnes said, in all their years of marriage. There was the weekend following their engagement.

Another time, many years ago, when they were driving back with the children from a holiday and stopped for a night on the way. The children stayed with their grandparents, while Pascal and Agnes went to the inn in town—a dreary, uncomfortable place, which Pascal nevertheless preferred to her parents' home.

Pascal's own mother and stepfather had little interest in being part of their lives, though they expressed some form of affection through lavish gifts—it was they who'd bought this apartment. They paid for the children's schools, their activities. The children never stayed with Pascal's parents alone, and perhaps Pascal took this as a standard by which other family relationships should be conducted. It had always baffled him that, in their healthier years, Agnes's parents offered to take the children for the whole summer. Sometimes, her parents stayed with the children for a week or two during the school term, so that Agnes and Pascal could travel together, though Pascal always preferred to arrange for a nanny rather than grandparents to take their place. It made him uncomfortable to be thankful, Agnes said, to have to depend on another person's care.

"That poor boy," Agnes's mother had once said, "is as fearful as a cat."

The candle cast a large shadow on the table, exaggerating the leaves of the wreath. Outside, the streetlamps were lit.

It was a decent life, Agnes said, that of her parents. She could say it now, because it seemed like the home of strangers, a movie she'd seen a long time ago. The decency was never called into question. Her parents could not understand the drama that shook others' lives daily. And even though they didn't judge these people—neighbors, friends, relatives—they'd lived with the relief of their own quiet existence.

It was important for her to remember this, in a time when everything was uprooted, dragged out of its foundations to be examined. These days, it seemed naïve to insist that there wasn't a problem; that a life could be led with harmony, without anything else concealed at its core.

When the children left for university, Agnes began to visit her parents weekly. She took the early morning train and arrived in their town in the afternoon. At the station, her father would be waiting for her on the platform and take her bag from her as soon as she stepped off.

They drove the short distance from town through the fields. Her father gripped the wheel with his large, bony hands, staring ahead.

At home, the three of them sat around the kitchen table. Agnes had returned there after so many years, after another life. She had been happy and unhappy, successful and adrift. She had become a painter, as she'd set out.

What story was Agnes telling me? How had she wandered here, in the monologue unraveling daily, without cease?

We were in the kitchen in the late evening. Agnes had come downstairs looking for me and I didn't know, by the time she started talking, how I could get up and leave.

Sitting in the dim kitchen of her parents' home, with the faint draft from the back door, the smell of damp and cooking, it would seem that nothing had changed in all those years and that she was the same person she had always been.

At dawn, she would hear her parents back in the kitchen, setting the table. Once her father sat down to eat, her mother went upstairs to change into her sitting clothes: a pale blue shirt, a beige skirt.

When Agnes's trips home became routine, they moved most of the furniture out of the dining room to make space for her work. A chair was placed by the window, where the walnut buffet had once stood. Her father painted over the stains on the walls, marking decades of their lives. Agnes set up her easel in the empty room, which was hallowed with the past, its dense, accumulated time now free to float in the cleared space.

The paintings she made in that room, she said, with their everyday mysticism, were her best works.

Her mother took off her slippers when she entered the dining room in the early morning so Agnes could paint her portrait. She sat down, her socks riding halfway up her thick ankles, leaving a sliver of flesh beneath her skirt. She read while Agnes prepared her palette. Then, she laid the book on her lap and crossed her hands over it, her eyes lowered. Her cheeks and mouth sagged softly.

Agnes didn't give her directions and they didn't talk as she painted. Her mother had once said that the hours of sitting soothed her, though at first it had been difficult to be looked at so closely by someone she loved.

The portrait took her a year to complete. The right side of her mother's face was haloed with light streaming from the window. Her body curved outwards with the bend of her back, echoing the small mound of her belly on which her eyes rested.

She must have been inspired by wooden statues of the Virgin, Agnes told me, those that are typically found in the north, whose dress is carved in widening waves around the breasts and between the legs.

Oh yes, she said, she had Pascal to thank for acquainting her with this stark art, with its strange, distorted humanity. But apart from these introductions, he'd been more or less absent from her work, in influence as well as emotion.

I thought she might say something more, just then, would tell me what was happening. But she only said that the painting of her mother was her own life's work. It was she who'd left and come back. And, she added bitterly, she'd been alone in her journey.

Everywhere, the city was lit, stocking up. Branches lined window frames, lights glittered in bakery fronts.

When I came back to the apartment from the library, I had a desire to take care of it. I wiped countertops, aired out blankets, washed the covers of the couches. I went to the market to buy flowers. I got up from my reading wanting to do something—to fold and wipe and air things out. Then I dimmed the lights and sat back down. All was heavy with the pleasure of waiting. Deep in the corners of homes; out on the streets and in shops. And in the apartment, too, there was the weight of anticipation.

Agnes was upstairs, lying for hours of the day in bed, then shuffling back and forth. When we ran into each other she looked apologetic, and greeted me briefly.

I still found gifts left for me on the kitchen table—desserts, wine, fruits. Another wreath for the kitchen, this one tied with a dark velvet ribbon. One morning there was an envelope full of money. A note inside explained that she and Pascal had decided to lower the rent. But even that, Agnes wrote, may not be enough to make up for her presence. I took the envelope, and wrote a note to thank her, which I left in front of the studio door. I considered adding that this was an unnecessary gesture, but finally decided against it.

For New Year's, I arranged to join three researchers from my university, to visit a town far south. I didn't know the others well but thought that the journey would be a welcome break. I didn't want to go back home—it would be too long a trip. Besides, it seemed appealing to be among near strangers. With the extra money from Agnes, I booked a hotel on the town's historic boardwalk, with a room overlooking the sea. In my note to Agnes, I'd written that I would be gone for the holidays. I didn't say where or how long. It had occurred to me fleetingly that if I provided details, Agnes might want to join as well, even though I had every reason to assume that she'd be spending this time with her family.

I left the apartment early one morning, when there was no sound from upstairs, closing the door softly behind me.

Over the holidays, I sent my adviser one more chapter on medieval attitudes towards the flesh and was taking some days off before I continued my work. I didn't quite believe my own argument that nudity served as an iconography of the soul—though it was a sturdy one, and well researched. More and more, it seemed to me that the flesh didn't signify nakedness at all, but was rather a sly cloak that concealed an inner—truly naked—meaning. As soon as I was back from the south, I took another trip to visit a church.

The building was unremarkable except for a calendar and zodiac, carved square by square on the western transept. At one time, it was believed that the twelve figures were those of the apostles, though there was no question that they represented the Labors of the Months.

The calendar started with images of feasts, roasting pigs, jugs of wine. In the following months, a figure sat huddled by a fire. He looked as though he had just stepped inside and taken off his shoes and was warming himself, still in his outdoor cloak. Early spring, when the earth began to thaw, a farmer stuck his shovel into the soil. Later, a cloaked traveler fed a bird standing in a field beneath capricious skies. As the season grew warmer, the traveler sat resting in the thick foliage of trees. Summer was illustrated with cutting and stacking, tending to the vines. Rest came after the harvest, the crushing of grapes and sowing of seeds. Then back again to the season of feasts, the seclusion of the cold months, the frozen soil.

It was a world that advanced with certainty, the sureness of the seasons, the promise of light and dark, cold and heat, water and grains, and with the confidence that it all meant the same thing to one's fellow humans.

She was sitting in the kitchen at dawn, wrapped in a smoke-colored robe. I'd woken up from the dream and lay in the dark for some time, unable to go back to sleep.

In the kitchen, everything was perfectly in place. The counters were empty, except for a paper bag with a loaf of bread I'd bought and left there the day before. The cream pitcher, the salt and pepper shakers, the glass of water I'd sipped before going to sleep stood huddled in shadows on the table.

She sat with her hands folded over her lap. Her hair was down, electrified on her shoulders. Her cheeks were luminous in the half-light. The rest of her thin body was folded into the gray of the morning.

How long had we not seen each other? How long had Agnes been living upstairs? I didn't even know whether she'd been in the apartment for the holidays and I didn't want to ask her. Out of respect, perhaps, or fear.

When she finally noticed me at the door, she nodded.

I asked if she'd like tea, or something to eat.

She shook her head, yes or no, I couldn't tell. I went to the stove to heat water. I took out butter and a jar of jam from the fridge. I began slicing the bread.

"Oh yes," I thought I heard her say, and turned to face her.

Until now, she said, she hadn't realized just how much her life at home got in the way of her work. She had many different projects in mind though she hadn't yet settled on a specific one.

"I've been doing very many things," she told me. "You mustn't think I'm doing nothing at all."

The kitchen walls shimmered gray. Agnes's face looked demented.

"Because it seems that you're avoiding me. I don't want you to feel that I'll trap you and take up all your time. I'm sorry to have put you in that situation." Still, she continued, staying here was the only way for her to proceed.

I kept silent.

She clutched the side of the table, as if we were on a boat. Besides, there was no reason for her to be at home. She hardly ever saw her husband these days. He was absorbed in his own life at the moment, she said.

When they did spend time together, it was always around an activity. She came along on his research trips, seeing nothing but rose windows and wreath columns for days on end. Other than that, their life was regulated by a cycle of social obligations. They could spend weeks in each other's company talking only to other people.

I took a bite of my toast. Agnes had buttered hers but had not touched it.

She mentioned their neighbors, a musicologist couple, with whom she and Pascal had spent at least an evening together weekly for the past two decades. At every gathering, they talked about concerts they'd attended, articles they'd read. They picked up hobbies and dropped them, always with an anecdote to deliver about the experience. Sometimes they all read the same book, for the sake of a discussion over dinner. Otherwise, Pascal invited varying groups of people into their lives, curated in matching activities and worldviews.

It went without saying that he was an impeccable host. He prepared the most casual event with attention, from the snacks they would serve before dinner to the drinks accompanying each episode of the evening.

Women often commented on his generous hosting. Wasn't Agnes so lucky, they said. Agnes was aware that her indifference to Pascal's hospitality endeared him to outsiders. They might even conclude that Pascal bore the burden of all the housework, that he sacrificed his own time to honor Agnes's. Still, Agnes didn't feel the need, after so many years, to pretend gratitude, when the dinners were not intended for her and she probably would not have hosted them in the first place. Nor did she go out of her way to explain that what the guests saw was not representative of their days; that Pascal cared for outsiders more than he ever had for his own family.

Still, Agnes said, she'd also benefited from the friendship of these people over the years. She took part in all of it, served to her on a platter.

But now that she was here, far from home, she realized that she had difficulty remembering these individuals who populated their lives.

"I keep asking what's left of me now, without all of that."

The sun had finally arrived, cloaking the kitchen in an even, pale light.

Agnes clutched the table once again. Sometime soon, she said, she hoped she would have a painting to show for her time here.

Already, it was spring.

I visited a church some hours east, with a spandrel relief of the creation narrative. In this depiction, Eve was not made from Adam's rib but was portrayed as one of his wings, as if the two had formed a celestial creature before they took their human shapes in Eden. The temptation was also depicted as a collaborative act, Adam and Eve standing curiously on either side of the tree, equal in their nudity, leaning their heads in to listen to what the serpent had to tell them. The unusual telling of the familiar story was inspired from the visions of a mystic, who'd written about it in vivid detail in a state of ecstasy.

Afterwards, I walked the town's streets, all of them leading back to the center square.

It was snowing when I came back to the city in the early evening, the first snow of the year, unexpected, unwelcome, and late. Leaving the train station, I heard a woman say that the world was spinning off its axis.

Outside, soft and steady flakes melted the moment they touched the ground. I moved for a while with the crowd, unable to find my bearings in the tangle of people, cars, and buses. Once I got onto the boulevard, the snow had picked up pace, slowly concealing the city from view. I stood on the curb, my hand raised, waiting for a taxi driver to see me.

The apartment smelled sweetly stale and I quickly discovered the source as the garbage I'd forgotten to take out; or perhaps I'd assumed that Agnes would do it.

I found a note from her on the kitchen table, telling me that she was leaving. Pascal had called and asked her to return. In her short note, she repeated this twice. Now that she was going home, because Pascal wanted her to come back, she might not even get to see me before my fellowship was over.

I walked the stairs to the studio and checked that the door was locked. Then I went back down to the kitchen. There was nothing in the fridge to eat. But I was relieved to be alone.

It took several moments after I was shaken awake before I identified the urgent sound at night as the phone. In my months at the apartment, I'd never heard the landline ringing.

"You're there," Agnes said. It had been several weeks since her departure. Already, the snow had turned to slush on the ground. There was no sign in her tone that she was aware of the hour. I asked if everything was alright.

"Suddenly," she said, "I find that my life has fallen apart."

Her voice was soft and steady. I asked what had happened.

"Oh, many things." She was coming to the city the next day.

I kept quiet.

"I'm so sorry," she said. "I'm sorry to bother you."

I left the apartment early the following morning to go to the archives. I'd been unable to fall asleep after the call. By dawn I'd given up trying. All day, I tried to focus on the dialogues of the rhetorician Minucius Felix. In his writings, he warned that impure spirits hid in statues and consecrated images, haunted temples, animated the entrails of animal sacrifices, guided the flight of birds, uttered prophesies steeped in lies.

When I came back to the apartment, the last of the afternoon light hung in a sturdy rope across the hallway. I went to the bedroom to leave my bags and change my clothes then sat on the bed for a while, my eyes closed, before going upstairs.

Agnes was sitting on the stool, wearing a heavy apron, cleaning brushes with a rag cloth. A large canvas was daubed in black and brown. Its purpose may have been to scrape off the paint from brushes, or to try out colors. She rose from the stool and kissed me on both cheeks, then sat down and resumed her cleaning.

I didn't ask about the phone call. I didn't know what to say. She was here, after all. Instead, I asked whether she'd finally found a new direction in her painting. She looked as if she didn't understand the question, and studied my face for several moments. She'd been trying to settle on a project, I reminded her, away from the obligations of her life at home.

"No," she said finally. "I haven't been thinking about any of that. I only came to the city because Pascal wanted us to spend time apart. Surely you must have realized that. You must have thought that something was wrong."

No, I said uneasily, I hadn't.

"It's difficult to tell," Agnes said, "whether you are exceedingly polite or willfully blind."

She'd been living in a fog this whole winter, waiting to go back home, trying to pass the time. And all these months, she hadn't considered the most obvious facts staring her in the face.

The rest of the story, she continued, was so banal that she barely had the energy to describe it.

Pascal had finally asked her to come back. These past weeks at home, he was kind and friendly and she supposed that the separation had been a good idea after all. He'd planned no dinners with acquaintances; instead he suggested that the two of them go for walks and to concerts. One evening, he took her to a restaurant in the mountains, perched on a cliff, a long drive from town. They'd been trying to go there for some time with their neighbors but hadn't managed before then to get a reservation.

Pascal told her about the booking some days in advance and asked her to keep the evening free. This was a detail, among many, that suffocated her in the aftermath of what had happened, leaving her with the cold fact of his calculations.

She'd worn a blue velvet dress, had gone that afternoon to the hairdresser. Pascal had no qualms about misleading her. He'd gone about his days in perfect calm. That same week, he'd prepared a roast. He bought tulips from the market. He asked for her opinion about two recordings of the same violin concerto.

What did a single week matter now, Agnes said, when the deceit was so much bigger? And yet it was these small events—the merry announcement of the reservation, her velvet dress, their car ride to the mountain—that pained her the most.

They arrived at the restaurant and took a table looking out at the mountains. The first course was a poached egg nestled in a bed of crisp leaves. An image of such fragility, Agnes said, that it kept flashing in her mind ever since. Pascal held her hand across the table—he'd pushed aside a vase and candle in order to do this—and told her that he had never, really, felt nurtured in their relationship. Agnes already knew this, he insisted; she probably shared his sentiment.

And they'd certainly done a good job of it, he said, living harmoniously for so many years, despite this.

As if to soothe her, he added that he'd only realized all this once he'd started seeing another woman some months earlier. She was warm and vibrant, and she made him feel a wealth of emotions he hadn't known he was capable of feeling.

They must have looked like couples in movies, Agnes said, the way they held hands across the table in candlelight.

When she could finally speak, Agnes said that she didn't understand. "You're holding my hand," she told him. "Why are you holding my hand?"

"You see?" Pascal said. This was a part of himself that was locked up during their marriage. He seemed to be saying that she was responsible for his imprisonment. But he was finally free now, and had emerged from the experience with compassion.

During the ride down the mountain, Agnes started to shiver. When she got home (Pascal dropped her off and, she assumed, went to the other woman's house) she could do nothing to warm herself. For several days after, she lay in bed with a hot water bottle. As she told me this, she lowered her eyes modestly, as if her temperature were the most intimate detail she could reveal about her body.

Then she picked up the rag from her knee and began cleaning her brushes once again.

Her children had arrived two days later. Their trip was planned months in advance, and in light of this, Pascal's timing struck her as all the more cruel.

They'd received the news from their father with surprise and sadness, they said; Pascal had told them on their ride from the airport. Within hours of being back, they'd settled into disorienting practicality as they would set to work on basic tasks. They wanted to take Agnes to the doctor to ask about her shivering. They made soup, following a recipe from one of their father's cookbooks. Her daughter proposed getting manicures, visiting the hairdresser together. "Just to get our minds off things," she said. Agnes wanted to explain to her that her mind was already off it—that it kept skidding across a smooth surface each time she tried to focus. What she needed was a way to get her mind on the subject, without slipping away, so that she could begin to understand.

They were upset with their father; they didn't want to see him for some time; they told Agnes repeatedly that they were sorry. But ultimately, they said, they didn't wish to take sides between their parents during their separation. That was their term for what was happening.

One evening—how many days had passed since their arrival?—Agnes shouted that it was deceit, that here was the full revelation of their father's character and it was outrageous to disguise it as anything else. But somehow it was she who appeared outrageous to her children.

One morning as they were having tea in the garden, wrapped in blankets, she tried once again to ask for her children's sympathy. Not taking sides, she told them, was a way to side with immoral behavior.

They wished their father had spoken to her sooner, her son said. More than this, they wished he hadn't sought fulfillment outside his own marriage. Her daughter sobbed as he said this. But ultimately, her son continued, what would really have changed in the grand scheme of things when, for whatever reason, the marriage had come to an end?

They would all go through the first painful months and grow accustomed to a new configuration of their family. It wasn't a matter of picking sides, he said, but figuring out how they could continue from here on.

Wasn't it at least good, her daughter said, having composed herself, that Agnes had moved to the city and finally had a chance to concentrate on her work?

Agnes had slid off the stool and was sitting on the floor.

Until then, she said, she'd always admired her children's

rational detachment from events that concerned others, as if this were proof of a superior constitution. To be sure, they were exemplary people—in their habits of consumption, their politics and donations and volunteer work. They lived their lives with textbook goodness. But they didn't know that goodness might take the form of harsh words, that anger might be the guardian of the weak.

Her children spent their entire trip with her. They canceled plans to see friends and travel to the mountains. They sat with her for hours, in the bedroom, the living room, the kitchen, out in the garden. They cooked and cleaned, bought flowers, put on music. Things they'd learned from her and Pascal, from the life they'd lived in that house. All this time, Agnes lay in a daze, moving from one room to the next.

On one of their last days, the children went on a walk with Pascal in the forest, upon his suggestion. Agnes couldn't understand their acquiescence. Before leaving the house, they made her tea, told her there was food in the fridge, assured her they would be back very soon, as if she were a child, or an invalid. They were back within a few hours. Agnes was on the couch, reading, and accepted the kiss her daughter planted on her forehead, as if checking for a fever. That evening, they asked her cautiously whether she would agree to having lunch with them and their father before they went back. It was such a strange question, Agnes said: the formality and restraint, the assumption that she would disagree with most of their proposals. No, it wasn't the type of care shown a child or invalid, but rather the attention practiced around the mentally ill.

They went to a new café in town, one that had been recommended to Pascal by one of his students. They talked about the children's work, their son's hiking trip, their daughter's plans for the summer. Agnes could tell that her children were relieved to be free from the shroud that had cloaked them those past days and chatted with enthusiasm. Madness, it occurred to her, was nothing more than the reversal of roles. And it was too much for any of them to bear.

The mad, she said, are those people who strip us of our conveniences and comforts.

When the food arrived, Pascal paused to gather their attention. He said, gravely, that he appreciated the children's maturity and support in this complicated moment for their family.

Just then, Agnes told me, she had the frightful sense that something terrible might happen to them all.

In May, with the heavy rains, the archives were closed for evacuation. The water rose higher, past the records of decades, past centuries. Cars disappeared into the river.

I'd made friends with several research fellows from different universities, whom I joined for drinks around the city and for dinners at the studios they were renting. Everyone brought something to contribute—wine, dessert, cheese—and we followed instructions from our hosts for chopping and preparing the foods before sitting down together for long meals lasting late into the night.

Following our last conversation, I'd asked Agnes whether she'd like me to find another place to stay, so she could have the apartment to herself.

"We agreed you'd be here until the summer," Agnes said.

"I intend to keep to our agreement." She added that the rent would remain lowered.

I related the situation to the other fellows and they all advised me to stay on. It would be too much work to look for a different place just then, though they agreed the situation was uncomfortable. It sounded, they said, as if my landlady was going through a very difficult time and could not even bring herself to act normally. It was also unfortunate, they agreed, that all this happened at such a critical period in my research, which would form the backbone of my doctoral work.

Coming home one afternoon, I found Pascal sitting in the kitchen. I gasped when I saw him.

"I'm sorry," he said. "I thought you were aware I'd be here."

He was tall and bulky with a tangle of dark hair. The features of his face protruded with character. The face of an artisan, I thought, or a monk. I hadn't imagined that he would look awkward, even cumbersome.

He got up from the chair and extended his hand.

"I'm sorry," he said again, by way of introduction.

He was in the city for a seminar and wanted to pick up some things from the apartment. He'd mentioned this to Agnes and they'd set a time when she would be out, so he had assumed that she would pass on the message. But it was quite possible that there'd been a miscommunication. He seemed to have a knack for misunderstanding her these days.

"I don't know when else I'll have a chance to come here," he said.

He was happy she was in the city, he added, and hoped that the change of scene would be good for her. He hoped, also, that her stay hadn't gotten in the way of my work.

How delightful, he continued, to have a colleague making use of the apartment. He'd actually been meaning to write me for months, but hadn't gotten a chance. Or rather, to be honest, he'd been unsure about meddling with this whole setup.

"I mean you and Agnes," he said. "I didn't want to get in the way of whatever the two of you decided. About sharing the space and so on. I thought I'd just let her communicate with you."

But it was a shame, he said, that he and I had not had a chance to talk. He had great admiration for my adviser, he continued. They didn't see as much of each other as they used to in the past but he followed her work closely. When I next spoke to her, I should make sure to pass on his regards.

"If you'll tolerate me for a bit longer, I'll just look through the bookshelves and be out of your way." He got up, and looked around at the kitchen cabinets, as if he expected to see the books there. Then he shrugged his shoulders in resignation.

I asked if he would like something to drink, though it was still quite early.

"I'd like nothing more," Pascal said.

I poured two glasses of white wine that Agnes had left for me in the fridge and brought the rest of the bottle to the living room, where Pascal was already examining the books.

He'd made a small pile beside him on the floor.

"I'll only pick a few that I really need," he said. "It makes me sad to take them away from this place." He was holding an old book of folk tales. He opened its gray cloth cover and ran his hand down its marbled first page. Then he closed it and put it back on the shelf. "She has such a knack for finding these things."

I might not know, he told me, that he and Agnes had lived in this apartment during the first years of their marriage. It had been a very different place then, certainly less refined, but full of their life together. Then, as now, it was Agnes who'd arranged everything, though not in the way of a young wife, with practicality and overt decorations. She had a horror of those types of homes, not unlike the home of her own parents, and had always said that she would rather live in cold austerity than in sentimental clutter. Pascal sometimes thought that all of Agnes's artistic sensibility was in reaction to her upbringing, to creating a life different from that of her parents.

Still, he went on, she managed to endow every place she entered with something of herself, faint and fragile. She was like a bird in everything that she did, collecting and dispersing, lining things up in an odd fashion.

If I'd ever seen Agnes's paintings, I would understand that they reflected this essential containment of her character, its nest-like quality. Her work was hypnotic for this reason, he said, and it revealed something profound about Agnes's interaction with the world, carefully enclosing her space and drawing boundaries.

"So, have you?" he asked. "Have you seen Agnes's paintings?"

I told him I'd seen one or two.

"And wouldn't you say that they're fascinating studies of containment? Their power, in my opinion, comes from what they don't reveal. Just like Agnes herself."

He came to sit at the edge of the couch and poured more wine in my glass and then in his. He looked at the bottle.

"Agnes's pick," he said.

Wasn't it true of all art, I asked, that its power lay as much in absence, in the deliberate choice of what was left out, as in what was revealed?

"Precisely," Pascal said, "but Agnes can't accept even this simple fact. She insists that my interpretation of her paintings has never been accurate."

Over the years, she'd become increasingly private about her work. Whether there was ambition at the root of it, or fear, he didn't quite know. Perhaps a resentment he'd never fully understood. Whatever the reason, she refused to let him into dialogue with her painting.

She'd been back home, as he was sure I knew, and had caused a storm wherever she went, telling anyone she happened to cross paths with about the details of their separation. It was surprising to hear that she was talking like this, as if to portray their marriage in a way that did not match the years they'd been together.

"You must have heard all about it."

Not really, I said.

She was upset, that much he could understand, but her constant refueling surely wouldn't relieve her pain.

In a few weeks, their children would come for their summer vacation and have a limited amount of time to spend with him and Agnes. On their previous visit, they'd devoted their days entirely to taking care of their mother. But they had many other people to see and were already exceedingly generous with the time they spared their parents. Besides, they'd been so accommodating, so levelheaded about the whole situation.

On the phone some days ago, Pascal suggested to Agnes that they should go on vacation together—just the four of them, of course, not his girlfriend, though he was eager for the children to get to know her. He proposed going to the sea, or to a small village in the mountains that Agnes adored. She'd been hostile, rejecting each proposal without consideration. Understandably so, maybe, but it wasn't unheard of that couples who'd parted ways after many years of marriage should remain friends, especially for the sake of the children.

"Anyway, she has every right," he said, crossing and uncrossing his legs. "This can't be an easy transition for her."

In the end, he'd asked Agnes to come up with any plan

she wanted, and he and his girlfriend would host the children for a few days in the time that remained. In response to his simple and, to his mind, rather generous suggestion, Agnes had dragged up some of the most distant episodes of their marriage. A monologue that lasted well into the night, while his girlfriend looked on, perplexed, from the adjacent room while he was trapped on the phone. The story Agnes had told him was a long and tortured one of their years together, of Pascal's blindness.

"Which is false," he said. "Of all my sins—and let's just say that I have many—blindness is certainly not one of them."

He was sensitive to her opinions nonetheless, he always had been. And perhaps because of this he'd allowed her to change the facts of the past, shifting them slyly, as imperceptibly as she changed the arrangement of a room.

From the very beginning, their relationship was founded on his admiration for her, his eagerness for the two of them to share a life. Anyone who'd known them for long enough would bear witness to this simple equation. Even if, he added, Agnes had dropped her friendships one by one, cutting her bonds with anything that tied her to the past. For each vanished relationship, she'd offer a different story of inevitability, but the truth was that she'd never allowed anyone to know her for long enough to let down her defenses. And over the years, she had twisted the story of their marriage into one of her own invisibility. She accused Pascal of being cold and insensitive. She found an intention of ill will in whatever he did, going far back to their happiest moments. It was impossible to disprove, he was aware, but he wasn't interested in proving anything.

He also had his girlfriend to consider in all this. She was a fierce woman, and had so far shown remarkable composure. But he was wary of taking her patience for granted.

"We're responsible for our own happiness," he said.

I put down my glass on the table and corked the bottle, to begin clearing up.

"Poor girl," Pascal said. "It makes me sad that she's doing this to herself. To be entirely honest with you, I don't think she's very balanced."

In fact, he continued, a few of their friends in town had recently approached him. Agnes was acting exceedingly strange, they said. She talked and talked, about anything and everything, no matter the setting.

"I admire your patience with her," he said. "I don't suppose it's been easy to cohabit."

I told him we got along without problem.

"I do hope she's been a little more considerate with you."

I reminded him, somewhat jokingly, of what he'd said in the kitchen, that he'd decided not to interfere with our setup. I added that I wanted to go out for a walk, and after that I needed to get some work done. If he was finished looking through the books, we could leave the apartment together.

"Listen," Pascal said, "I know what you're thinking: Agnes is abandoned. Her husband left her for another woman. He has no sympathy for her pain.

"Isn't that so?" he asked. "Isn't that exactly what you think? Oh, the same old story."

I supposed so, I told him.

He placed the books in a cloth bag, then looked around one last time. Then he went back into the living room and took the tree painting off the bookshelf. He held it up and put it into his bag.

I asked whether he'd told Agnes he would be taking it.

"I beg your pardon," Pascal said. "You seem to forget that I'm in my own home."

His large, soft face was blotched crimson.

"You wouldn't even know," he said, "that this was a present from me. When I got her this painting, she was very upset. We'd seen it at a gallery and we both loved it. But when I bought it and gave it to her, she found it excessive. She said that if I really wanted to make her happy, I could've asked her. That's what she can be like, getting angry at a present, but you probably haven't seen this side of her."

He was at the door now, holding it open for me. I stepped out.

"As a matter of fact," he said, "it might please her that I took the painting. Because she loves to feel righteous. She's been right all these years, in all the decisions she's made and those she hasn't. But can it really be that she alone has a moral compass that is denied the rest of us?"

He locked the door. "Do you have your own keys?" he asked. "I won't be coming back." I nodded.

We walked down the stairs, but before we reached the ground floor, Pascal paused.

"You know," he said, "you have to wonder about the possibility that someone is always purer than you are, at every instance, that they've been disappointed by you again and again. Not out of any fault of their own, of course not, but because of all your own shortcomings, of your countless insensitivities. Just think about what it would be like to live with someone like this."

I waited for him to continue.

"I have to say I'm a bit upset about our conversation," he said. He took a step down, then paused again. I took a step as well.

"This whole time, you've let me go on and on without offering a single word of understanding.

"You're probably just waiting for me to be off so you can get on with your evening. None of this concerns you, of course. You're just a tenant. You only want to have a place to get your work done. But I hoped for a little recognition, some feedback. Even if you were to tell me that you disagree with my assessment of the situation. It's a human response, after all, even if you don't owe us anything.

"After all," he said, "a young and intelligent . . . sensitive . . ."

He raised his hand and slowly placed it on my shoulder. It was strong, heavy.

I thought for a moment that he might push me.

The hallway light suddenly went out and we stood for some seconds in darkness.

Then, holding on to the railing, we walked down the last steps and paused in front of the main door. Pascal went before me and held the brass knob. Finally, he pulled it open.

The evening air was warm and fragrant. The trees on the

street were in bloom. I was struck by the freeing sensation of being outside.

Pascal pushed the bag farther up on his shoulder. He hoped, he said, that I would convey his best regards to my adviser.

Mornings, the apartment expanded with light. Light flitted across the walls and curtains, streaked the floorboards, lay dappled on the sheets, as if a luminous brush
had left its mark upon my awakening.

From my bed, I could see the small, trellised balcony, lush
again with thick foliage and purple flowers of a clematis
climbing up one wall. White geraniums lined the railing.

In the year that I lived there, I had the sense of having
stepped inside another life.

In June, I read of the discovery of a pilgrim's letters during his travels to the country's northern cathedrals. The pilgrim's description of the nude sculptures was frank and sympathetic, without any squeamishness or avoidance of the subjects' sex, nor with any hint of judgment towards the fallen bodies.

Unlike the widely held belief among art historians that the naked body was a topic of evasion for medieval men and women, the letters suggested that perhaps it held a comfortable place, even central, in the Gothic imagination.

Before my return, I would take a final trip to the municipal archives where the letters were held. From there, I would go back to my university, once I sorted out my housing for the following semester.

In the final weeks of my stay, I heard furniture being dragged upstairs, scraping the floor. One time, there was a large, white canvas propped against the wall in the hallway. Several days later, it was gone.

One day I found a note on my door telling me that Agnes would be in the studio if I wished to join her for a bite.

She was sitting on the stool, the bones of her face jutting out in a frenzied geometry. Her yellow eyes were feverish.

The large canvas I'd seen in the hallway the previous week took up the entirety of a wall. Vague figures seated around a table were sketched in ochre. On the floor were several smaller canvases, with similar sketches.

The table was set with small and large bowls, cutting boards topped with food. The cream pitcher from the kitchen held a bouquet of purple thistles. There was a bottle of wine, a lit candle.

"Thank you for coming," Agnes said, getting up to hug me. Her long arms reached behind me hesitantly, not fully pressing on my back. "It's good to be with a friend."

She looked at me quickly, to see my reaction. I told her it was great to see her, and I meant what I said; I would be leaving soon.

In one corner of the studio was a pile of branches, high enough that they looked like an animal's dwelling.

"I walked all the way to the woods last week," she said, lifting a sinewy branch. "Look how beautiful this is."

On one side of the table, beside the food, were more drawings and books.

I picked up the sketch on top, a charcoal of a hand at the edge of a table, surrounded by cups and plates.

Agnes opened a heavy book to a painting of the disciples seated around a long table. The sketch I was holding was a reproduction of a small detail from the painting. The hand rested on the folded surface of cloth beside an empty plate, and beyond it a clutter of other cups and plates. When separated from the rest of the composition, it had a different significance, more solitary, communicating anticipation, even anxiety, for the invisible meal.

"I've always been drawn to the idea of a last supper," Agnes said. "The deliberation of it, as well as the resignation to fate."

These days, she said, she spent many hours looking at the paintings of the old masters. She recognized in them not just beautiful works, as she used to, but the strain of a deep and steady vision. Their honesty moved her, but she realized that this honesty was often overlooked, in favor of other aspects of their work. Their style and innovation, for example, or, as she'd just said, their beauty.

She motioned for me to sit on a cushion on the floor. She brought me a glass of wine and a plate with food. It was filled with spreads of different colors, smoked fish, cheeses, a round, golden pastry. I wondered when she had prepared all of this. She went back to the table and picked up another plate and filled that, too. She pulled her stool towards me and sat down. We raised our glasses.

"It's good of you to come," she said again. "It's good to be with a friend."

I had the feeling she was testing out the word, the new relationship, to see if I might object.

"I believe you met my husband."

I'd been here briefly when he came, I said, adding that I hadn't known he'd be taking things from the apartment. I told him explicitly, I informed Agnes, that I wasn't comfortable with this and that he should ask for Agnes's permission.

"Don't worry about that." Agnes smiled. "I didn't expect that you'd stop him."

I remembered my first impression of her, how charismatic she'd been.

"Besides," she said, "I assume he found a way to make me seem heartless."

I examined the sketch I'd placed beside me. Did she intend to use these studies for her new canvas, I asked.

"Not really," she said.

Recently, she'd begun to remember bits and pieces of a childhood episode involving one of her cousins. Stories she thought had left her life without a trace came back to strike her with the realization of their strangeness, though the strangeness had been ignored at the time, or people had somehow carried on, adapting and adjusting, without naming the abnormality.

This cousin, she continued, who presently occupied her thoughts but whom she hadn't thought about in years, had been an important figure in Agnes's childhood. She was only a few years older than Agnes, but she'd had an entirely different upbringing, devoid of rules. She was allowed to eat in her room, for example, listening to music. She had a way of talking to her parents, at once ladylike and capricious, as if she were a celebrity, with a fully developed sense of her own needs and preferences. Her clothes were fashionable, unlike the modest ones that Agnes's mother insisted on. She wore short skirts, put on earrings and nail polish. The thrill of seeing her cousin was in part the discovery of what new style she'd taken up. Agnes would spend the days in between their visits trying to guess, though the reality was always something more surprising than what she had imagined.

Throughout her childhood, and especially as she got older and moved closer towards her own individuality, Agnes felt embarrassed around her cousin because of her plain clothes and her family's old-fashioned ways. This didn't propel her into any action, nor did she pretend to be other than she was, at least not then. She took it as a fact that her parents appeared ordinary and provincial from the outside: frugal and traditional, living in parallel to the changing world but unaffected by it.

When the families visited each other, the girls went to the bedroom to listen to music and try out hairstyles and outfits. As much as she loved the visits, Agnes often felt that she was a burden and was taking up her cousin's time when she would certainly have preferred to be out with her friends. But her cousin never showed boredom and was always engaged, each time inventing endearing names for her. Even then, Agnes could not let go of the feeling that her cousin would rather be elsewhere. Nor did it occur to her that the cousin also might have looked forward to their visits.

The families saw each other regularly in Agnes's childhood and adolescence. Then came a period when the visits grew sparse, perhaps because of the girls' demanding studies. Agnes often thought about her cousin, wondering what new trends she might have picked up and which she'd already abandoned. Agnes's own choices were always subjected to what she imagined were her cousin's opinions. The cousin was both real and fictional to her—an embodiment of all that Agnes wanted to be, fashioned from the particular details of her cousin's tangible self.

"We form ourselves through our doubles," Agnes said, looking towards the stairs. "We make ghostly twins to carry the weight of our desires."

When Agnes was in high school, the cousin's father died suddenly and left the family with nothing. It had seemed to Agnes and her parents that the cousin's family lived more or less as they did—modestly and responsibly—but it turned out that they'd been living from one day to the next, spending their money on insignificant things, without a thought for the future or for establishing security in their lives. The mother had to borrow from relatives, take work cleaning houses. This was what Agnes remembered most from the time of the uncle's death, and very little about the tragedy itself.

People could be cruel when faced with suffering, she said, especially when it looked messy. It was easy to see the situation as a loss of dignity, only because it was uncomfortable to look at.

She was still holding her plate and wineglass, the contents of both untouched. She leaned over and placed the plate on the edge of the table.

"You must be wondering what you've gotten yourself into here," she said to me. "You must have been wondering all this time. After all, you were only here to do your own work."

I asked what had happened to the family.

The cousin and her mother slowly retreated within themselves. They, too, were embarrassed; no one made an effort to draw them out.

When Agnes next saw the cousin some years later, the girl was shockingly overweight, without a hint of her old spark or confidence. She'd lost her charisma as surely as if it were a coat she'd taken off.

But nothing had changed in her tenderness towards Agnes; she remembered the pet names she'd called her and the times the two of them used to sit in her room and listen to music.

She had the feeling, Agnes said, that her cousin was made up of separate parts that could be assembled and disassembled. She had taken off one piece but kept another.

It was around this time that Agnes decided to start

painting and soon afterwards moved to the city, where she took on a poised character. There was no other word for it, she said, the *taking on*—an act that gradually became her. She'd learned to display her femininity and charm, and to hint at them through concealment. And even though she hadn't considered it at the time, it was obvious that the person she was imitating, when she moved to the city, was the idea of her cousin in her carefree years.

In those days, Agnes said, she had a sense of her own power as a sort of magnet, a hidden mass she could summon whenever she wanted. She knew neither its true dimensions nor its properties, only that she could call on it and it would come through, endowing her with charisma. Did I remember, for example, her story about the instructor she'd seduced at art school? I nodded.

Things went smoothly for her during that period. Not just the early success of her paintings and her marriage, but daily encounters when she had the sense of molding and expanding people's admiration, of teasing them with little compliments and receiving theirs in return.

"I was such a charming girl," she said blankly.

She still remembered the belief in her own invincibility, her shocking confidence. And she wondered whether it didn't have something to do with the demise of her role model, which may have given her the permission to step fully into her character.

"But no," she added after a moment's consideration. "That would be going too far. Because the truth is that I barely thought about her. She had already become insignificant to me."

She realized that this was a monstrous thing to say.

In the following years, she heard news that her cousin had become increasingly reclusive. She rarely left the house, and after a while not at all. Later, she didn't leave her room if there was anyone at home besides her mother. Gradually, she began staying in the room for days at a time, the same one where she and Agnes had played together as children, its walls covered with posters of actors.

After some time, the death of the uncle had been all but forgotten and the tragedy that hovered over the family was that of the daughter. It often happened, Agnes said, that we saw only the misshapen offspring of trauma, while we grew blind to the events that had given birth to it in the first place.

Many years ago, before her parents had died, Agnes went with them to call on the cousin and her mother. She was already married then, and too preoccupied to pay attention to anything other than the events of her and Pascal's lives. The trip home had been a short one, while Pascal was away at a conference.

They arrived with chocolates and a bottle of cognac Agnes had brought with her from the city. They were meant as presents for her parents, but most of the gifts she brought them were passed on to other acquaintances. Her parents always told her there was nothing they needed and perhaps they even thought that her extravagant presents were frivolous.

At first the cousin only called out to them from behind the door of her room, but after a while she emerged and sat with them for an hour, which was something, her mother informed them, she'd never done before, at least not since her complete reclusion.

She was enormous, Agnes said, a woman-child of incredible proportions. She walked slowly, in a long, white cotton gown. Her skin was shockingly pale, so much that it seemed to glow. She smiled at them joyfully, and clapped her hands when she saw Agnes, but she didn't hug them or come too close. They'd heard from relatives that she had developed a sort of phobia—of germs, perhaps, if not something more abstract—and this may have been one of the reasons she didn't usually leave her room. She sat next to her mother, and the two of them talked giddily, finishing each other's sentences and showering their visitors with affection. After Agnes and her parents were served coffee, the cousin was brought hers on a different tray. She took the cup from her mother's unsteady hand, squeezing the old woman's arm.

"Thank you, darling," she told her. They were like spinster sisters in fairy tales, their kindness teetering on strangeness.

I glanced behind Agnes at the canvas taking up the wall. Among the rough figures of people seated around the table was the large shape of a woman in a long shirt, her unruly hair descending to her waist.

But remembering them now, Agnes said, this mother and daughter who had once been very close to her and yet were still strangers, what unsettled her most was the reversal of fortunes. She didn't know whether her cousin might have become equally reclusive if her father had lived, or if she would have taken a similar turn regardless. In any event, Agnes was not blameless, she felt. She'd avoided her relatives—not overtly, that much was true, but she did not go out of her way to visit or call them. It was a wish to keep herself clean from their ungainly suffering. She'd let the matter go, and all she could say in her defense was that she felt guilt whenever she thought about her cousin over the years.

The light had drained from the studio. The candle on the table cast a shadow against the wall, and the canvas. In the soft obscurity, Agnes's face appeared smooth and distorted—her forehead wide, swallowing her feverish eyes, her mouth protruding beneath her nose. It was the face of an animal, I thought, a creature without human expression, though all the more alive with a meaning I could not decipher.

When her parents were alive, Agnes would receive news of her cousin from her mother, who continued to call the family on New Year's and birthdays. They always asked after Agnes, her mother told her, and were delighted by the developments in her life—her marriage, her children, her travels and work. Her mother had sent them the catalog of Agnes's first gallery show and relayed the cousin's remark that she'd found the paintings sad. At the time, Agnes hadn't given much thought to this remark. Her parents had not been to the gallery show, either, probably because they didn't want to intrude.

In any case, this secondhand communication with the cousin had ended with her parents' passing, and Agnes had had no news of the family in years.

"But what I realize now," she said, "is that they were not ungainly at all."

She wanted desperately to learn how they managed to make a life for themselves. It seemed impossible, she continued, that they'd been so quiet, that they hadn't come asking for help or begging for company.

"The thing is," she said, "I suddenly feel in need of sympathy, and I don't know where to seek it."

I wanted to respond to her, to defend myself.

She felt that she was coming unhinged, Agnes continued. She had an urge to cause harm whenever she noticed people acting insincerely. She wanted to confront them— perfect strangers, even—with what she thought was the banality of their lives. The only people who seemed to escape her wrath were the truly suffering, who had no energy for pretense. Those people, she said, who stood naked among us and made no fuss of their humiliation.

She got up from the stool and switched on the light. The table and the canvas, the piles of paper on the bed, awakened in an instant.

It was then that I noticed the faces of the figures seated around the woman in the long white shirt. In the empty stares of all the guests gathered around her, in their round eyes and pursed lips, their cheeks drained of color, I recognized the features—relentless and repeating—of my own face.

Agnes sat back down, picked up her plate, and brought an olive to her mouth, watching me.

What did this mean? I asked her, getting to my feet. I stepped closer to the canvas for a better look. The faces were demented, deformed, inhuman, with the twisted expressions of gargoyles.

What was this supposed to mean? I repeated.

"Does it offend you?" Agnes asked. "Because from all our months of living together, I got the impression that you weren't one to be easily moved."

This painting, I told her, was abnormal. It was intentionally, cruelly distorted.

"It's just a painting," Agnes said. "Maybe not a very beautiful one, but it's hardly something to ruffle you."

She tilted her head, examining my face.

"I see so much of myself in you," she said. "Your reserve, your elegant detachment. The way you've set out to succeed. And your flawless aesthetics, of course, if I may flatter myself with the comparison. I know how much work it requires to strip your life of everything unwieldly."

She turned again to look at the canvas.

She was waiting to see what would come through, she said. She had so much in store for it. She felt something rising steadily inside her. It might erupt suddenly, or it might be a slow, burning spill.

For now, she could only imagine the damage it would cause and what would remain in its wake.

# Acknowledgments

My heartfelt thanks to Karl Whittington for suggesting the narrator's research topic and generously sharing reading material. Any mistakes regarding the Gothic field are my own.

Thank you Fuat Savaş, Vera Schoeller, Zsófia Young, Kavita Bedford, Zachary Fox for your readings and suggestions. Thank you also, Zach, for the photograph, and the continued conversations and retreats. Thank you to the Voltaire group for your insightful feedback on the au pair chapter.

Thank you Cressida Leyshon and *The New Yorker* for publishing an early chapter and for your acute sensitivity to the text.

Sarah Bowlin, Laura Perciasepe, Cal Morgan, and the team at Riverhead: thank you for your support and for bringing the book to life.

Deep gratitude to my husband and first reader, Maks Ovsjanikov, for sharing every challenge and every joy.